PENGUIN BOOKS

GRAY HEROES

Jane Yolen, author of over two hundred published books, has been called the "Hans Christian Andersen of America" (*Newsweek*) and the "Aesop of the twentieth century" (*New York Times*). A storyteller, poet, critic, novelist, children's-book writer, and college teacher, she is also a wife, mother, and grandmother, all roles she plays with great gusto. Her previous folklore collection, *Favorite Folktales from Around the World*, is a favorite with teachers and storytellers. Her prizewinning children's books, such as *Owl Moon*, *Sleeping Ugly*, and *The Devil's Arithmetic*, are mainstays in the classroom. Her books and stories have won innumerable awards, including the Caldecott Medal, the Nebula, three Mythopoeic Society awards, a nomination for the National Book Award, the Christopher Medal, the Society of Children's Book Writers and Illustrator's Golden Kite Award, and many other honors. She has received five bodies-of-work awards and two honorary degrees. She is sixty years old. Or young. Depending on how you look at it.

Gray Heroes

Elder Tales from
Around the World

EDITED BY

Jane Yolen

Penguin Books

PENGUIN BOOKS

Published by the Penguin Group

Penguin Putnam Inc., 375 Hudson Street,
New York, New York 10014, U.S.A.
Penguin Books Ltd, 27 Wrights Lane,
London W8 5TZ, England
Penguin Books Australia Ltd, Ringwood,
Victoria, Australia
Penguin Books Canada Ltd, 10 Alcorn Avenue,
Toronto, Ontario, Canada M4V 3B2
Penguin Books (N.Z.) Ltd, 182–190 Wairau Road,
Auckland 10, New Zealand

Penguin Books Ltd, Registered Offices:
Harmondsworth, Middlesex, England

First published in Penguin Books 1999

10 9 8 7 6 5 4 3 2 1

ISBN 0 14 02.7618 1

(CIP data available)

Printed in the United States of America
Set in Centaur
Designed by Jennifer Daddio

This book is for Milbre Burch,
my dear storytelling friend

With special thanks to
Leeyanne Moore, Lois Ward Royal,
and Barbara Lipke for their help

Contents

Wisdom

Trickery

Adventure

And a Little Bit of Love

Introduction

I

My first gray hair appeared when I was twenty-four. Proudly I displayed it at the publishing company where I worked as an editor. The secretary, thinking she was doing me a favor, pulled the gray hair out before I could stop her.

"There!" she said. "Now no one will ever know."

No one would ever know what? That I was growing older? Getting on? Falling apart? Going downhill? Setting foot on the downward slope? Proceeding headlong into winter? Plunging into feebleness, infirmity, senility, and old age? Or, in

Shakespeare's words, "fall'n into the sere, the yellow leaf"?

Or perhaps she meant that no one would know that I was in fact maturing, ripening, flowering, mellowing, tempering, gaining wisdom, growing in stature, hitting my prime, "coming into my estate."

Years later, when I discovered the following folktale—Korean, Arabic, Aesopian, take your pick—I was reminded of that moment with my secretary.

OLD MAN, YOUNG MISTRESS

There was an old man who had a young mistress, though he was careful to keep it a secret.

"You look so old," she told him, and so he allowed her to pluck out all his white hair.

His wife saw how his white hair was disappearing, and guessed he was having an affair. She beat her breast and cried that he was deceiving her.

"Never!" he protested. And to prove his innocence, he let his wife pull out his black hair.

In this way, the old man was soon bald.

Of course nowadays no one will ever know how much white hair I have. Or how much black. Or if in fact I am completely bald. In the twentieth century nature has been overtaken by chemistry, surgery, and artifice. (To be fair, wigs and makeup have been around for as long as humans have cared about such things.) I am a grandmother by year count, but look nothing like my own grandmothers, who were white-haired, wrinkled, and slow. They had expansive bosoms and comfortable laps, and always wore cotton flower-print dresses. My strongest memories of them come from the time I was a young child—and they were in their late fifties!

These days the ski slopes are full of grandmothers. And grandfathers. They whiz past their slower children, whose caution is dictated by awesome responsibilities. Or they join Elderhostel for new learning experiences, go on trips planned for older constituencies, or on bike rides across the country.

The gracefully retired seem tireless, have time and means and more life ahead of them than ever before. According to a recent news report, there were 1,500 U.S. centenarians in 1962, 50,000 in 1995, and a projected one million in 2050. In fact a report from the American Census Bureau forecasts that people over 85 will become the fastest-growing age group by the middle of the twenty-first century.

Of course, few of us are likely ever to reach the ages of the biblical greats. The Old Testament cites Abraham as 100 when his son Isaac was born, who himself went on to live until 175. Abraham's wife, Sarah, died at 125. Methuselah— the oldest of the biblical crew—reputedly lived to 969. Even allowing for quite a bit of hyperbole, there were ancients in those days. Still, older folk are going to become more and more common in our society in the years ahead, and that change will naturally bring with it a brand-new set of political, economic, and cultural problems.

But folklore has already dealt with this phenomenon. In the following Norwegian tale, the housing situation, at least, has been solved.

THE SEVENTH FATHER OF THE HOUSE

There was once a man who was travelling. He came, at last, to a beautiful, big farm. It had a manor house so fine that it could easily have been a small castle.

"This will be a good place to rest," he said to himself as he went in through the gate. An old man, with grey hair and beard, was chopping wood nearby.

"Good evening, father," said the traveller. "Can you put me up for the night?"

"I'm not the father of the house," said the old one. "Go into the kitchen and talk to my father."

The traveller went into the kitchen. There he found a man who was even older, down on his knees in front of the hearth, blowing on the fire.

"Good evening, father. Can you put me up for the night?" said the traveller.

"I'm not the father of the house," said the old fellow. "But go in and talk to my father. He's sitting by the table in the parlor."

So the traveller went into the parlor and talked to the man who was sitting by the table. He was much older than both the others, and he sat, shivering and shaking, his teeth chattering, reading from a big book almost like a little child.

"Good evening, father. Will you put me up for the night?" said the man.

"I'm not the father of the house, but talk to my father who's sitting on the settle," said the old man who sat by the table, shivering and shaking, his teeth chattering.

So the traveller went over to the one who was sitting on the settle, and he was busy trying to smoke a pipe of tobacco. But he was so huddled up, and his hands shook so that he could hardly hold onto the pipe.

"Good evening, father," said the traveller again. "Can you put me up for the night?"

"I'm not the father of the house," replied the huddled up old fellow. "But talk to my father who's lying in the bed."

The traveller went over to the bed, and there lay an old, old man in whom there was no sign of life but a pair of big eyes.

"Good evening, father. Can you put me up for the night?" said the traveller.

"I'm not the father of the house, but talk to my father who's lying in the cradle," said the man with the big eyes.

Well, the traveller went over to the cradle. There lay an ancient fellow, so shrivelled up that he was no bigger than a baby. And there was no way of telling there was life in him except for a rattle in his throat now and then.

"Good evening, father. Can you put me up for the night?" said the man.

It took a long time before he got an answer, and even longer before the fellow finished it. He said—he like all the others—that he was not the father of the house. "But talk to my father. He's hanging in the horn on the wall."

The traveller stared up along the walls, and at last he caught sight of the horn, too. But when he tried to see the one who was lying in it, there was nothing to be seen but a little ash-white form that had the likeness of a human face.

Then he was so frightened that he cried aloud: "GOOD EVENING, FATHER! WILL YOU PUT ME UP FOR THE NIGHT?"

There was a squeaking sound up in the horn like a tiny tit-

*mouse, and it was all he could do to make out that the sound
meant: "Yes, my child."*

*Then in came a table decked with the costliest dishes, and
with ale and spirits, too. And when the traveller had eaten and
drunk, in came a good bed covered with reindeer hides. And he
was very glad that at last he had found the true father of the
house.*

If a great portion of the population is elderly, how will
we then define old age? A recent survey of baby boomers in-
dicated that they already thought old age begins at 79.

Or, as Bernard Baruch once wrote, "Old age is fifteen
years older than I am."

II

Once the storytellers were the ancients, who like great skin
containers, held the wine of story for their communities.
They doled it out, sip by sip: history, mystery, lineage, and
law. They were both entertainment and enrichment. They
carried wisdom in the mouth, adventure on the tongue.

They told stories by the campfire, by the child's bedside,
at the king's knee. They told stories in temple, in church, in
meetings, in rituals, on holidays, and to explicate a point
of law.

In order to remember all the stories they needed to tell,
they had to collect and learn the tales over many long years.
The apprenticeship of storytellers was often measured in
numbers of stories. For example, the Irish poet-tellers, who

had to be wise in philosophy, astronomy, and magic, also had to know 250 prime tales as well as 100 subsidiary ones. No wonder storytellers were ancient. It takes a long time to learn that many tales. As it is said in Tibet: "Better than the young man's knowledge is the old man's experience."

So, given that the old ones were once the main tale tellers, why are there so few stories starring the elderly?

Actually, there are a great many more than most of us realize. Somewhere along the way to the twentieth century, however, a good number of those tales were hidden, buried, put away on a top shelf.

The ancients are not the only storytellers today. There has been an incredible renaissance of storytelling in the last twenty years in America, in Europe, and in Japan. What was once the province of the shanachie, the griot, the biwa hoshi, or the patriarchs and matriarchs of a tribe or society has become a vital and popular art form. Storytelling workshops and performances in nontraditional settings such as hospital wards, prisons, coffeehouses—and even in senior centers and nursing homes—have become the ordinary, not the rare. What used to take centuries of traveling from mouth to ear over and over again now gets transferred across the nations and cultures by television, by audiotapes, by jet-setting tellers going from place to place. What was described by Joseph Campbell as "the long attrition of time, traversing the familiar boundaries of language and belief," the period in which a tale underwent (again in Campbell's words) "kaleidoscopic mutations," is now done over a weekend at a storytelling conference, or in an hour on E-mail.

But more important than the teller has been the resituating of the tales. In the last couple of centuries, folk stories got moved into the nursery because more and more people became literate. As life became technological and complicated, such tales seemed fit only for children. And children, of course, wanted to hear stories about other children, or about adventurous and romantic young adults. None of this *old people* stuff.

So the only stories starring graybeards that were saved for the nursery were the ones in which the child character assumed more importance than the elderly one.

Typical of this shift is the following Grimm's tale, which has counterparts across the world:

THE OLD MAN AND HIS GRANDSON

There was once a very old man, whose eyes had become dim, his ears dull of hearing. When he sat at table, he could hardly hold the spoon, and spilt the broth upon the table-cloth or let it run out of his mouth. His son and his son's wife were disgusted at this, so the old grandfather at last had to sit in the corner behind the stove, and they gave him his food in an earthenware bowl, and not even enough of it. He used to look towards the table with his eyes full of tears. Once, too, his trembling hands could not hold the bowl, and it fell to the ground and broke. The young wife scolded him, but he said nothing and only sighed. Then they bought him a wooden bowl for a few half-pence, out of which he had to eat.

They were once sitting thus when the little grandson of four years old began to gather together some bits of wood upon the ground. "What are you doing there?" asked the father. "I am making a little trough," answered the child, *"for father and mother to eat out of when I am big."*

The man and wife looked at each other for a while, and presently began to cry. Then they took the old grandfather to the table and henceforth always let him eat with them, and likewise said nothing if he did spill a little of anything.

Though this tale seems to be about the old man and what infirmities age has plagued him with, the story is really about the wisdom of the ingenuous child. An Irish variant of the story deals with a blanket cut in half. The Mexican tale deals with half a rug. The Korean version involves a pack-carrier in which the aged grandfather has been carried out into the woods. But no matter the cultural differences, the core of the story remains the same. In each instance, it is the open-natured child, innocent of the lessons he is expounding, and free of the ironies with which the tale is rife, who changes both his father and mother's—and the reader's—perceptions of old age.

Honoring thy father and mother, the tale warns, is a precept often easier to follow when mother and father are not drooling and incontinent.

There are to be sure close cousins of that story in which the young child has been left out. In these tales it is the elderly parent's wisdom (or the memory of what the aged parent had meant to the family) that makes the difference. But these stories are not anywhere near as popular or widespread as "The Old Man and His Grandson" and have survived mostly only in Far Eastern cultures.

One such story, from eleventh-century Japan, follows.

MOUNTAIN OF ABANDONED OLD PEOPLE

In ancient times there prevailed a custom of abandoning old people when they reached the age of sixty. Once an old man was going to be abandoned on a mountain. He was carried there in a sedan chair by his two sons. On the way the old man broke the branches of the trees. "Why do you do such a thing? Do you break the branches in order to recognize the way to come back after we leave you on the mountain?" asked the sons. The old father just recited a poem!

> *"To break branches in the mountain*
> *Is for the dear children*
> *For whom I am ready to sacrifice myself."*

The brothers did not think much about their father's poem, and took him up the mountain and abandoned him. "We shall go another way to return home," they said, and started on the way back.

The sun set in the west, but they could not find the way home. Meanwhile the moon came up and shone on the mountain. The two sons had no recourse but to return to their father. "What have you been doing until now?" he asked. "We tried to go back by a different way, but we could not get home. Please kindly tell us the way." So they carried the father again and went down the mountain, following their father's instructions, according to where he had broken the branches. When the brothers returned home, they hid their father under the floor. They gave him food every day and showed their gratitude for his love.

Some time afterward the lord issued a notice to the people to make a rope with ashes and present it to him. The people tried to make a rope by mixing ashes and water but no one could do it. Then the two brothers talked about this to the old father. The father said: "Moisten straw with salty water and make a rope of the straw; then after it is dried, burn it and present the ashes to the lord in the shape of a rope."

The brothers did just as he told them and presented the ash-rope to the lord. The lord was much pleased and said: "I feel very secure in having such wise men in my country. How is it that you possess such wisdom?" The two brothers explained in detail about their father. The lord heard them out, and then gave notice to all the country that none should abandon old people thereafter. The two brothers returned home with many rewards, which delighted the old father.

The place where the old father was abandoned is said to be Obasuteyama, the Mountain of Abandoned Old People.

Interestingly enough, the stories about age and usefulness that have been kept the most current in the popular folk mind are not tales about old people at all, but about old hounds, old horses, and other household or farmyard beasts who have outlived their usefulness. The four animals in the classic Grimm tale "The Musicians of Bremen" are a prime example. About to be killed because they have grown old, the cat, dog, donkey, and rooster go off together to make up a traveling band. Along the way they show that their courage and ingenuity have not deserted them in their antiquity. This "old dog outliving usefulness" motif, in which a faithful old dog, grown decrepit, is to be killed by his master, is so popular that it has its own number (Motif B842, Type 101) in the folklore motif index, that great academic repository of tale types. The Grimms called the story "Old Sultan," the Ukrainians "Old Dog Sirko," and in Aesop the story is simply "The Old Hound."

Less familiar, perhaps, but certainly well traveled, is the following tale from Italy, "The Bell of Atri," which deals in its own way with the same problem of the faithful animal— this time a horse—who has grown old.

THE BELL OF ATRI

Long ago, there was a town in Italy called Atri. Because the people desired harmony and justice, they hung a large bell in the center of the town. The people said, "Anyone who has been wronged can ring the bell. We will all gather and settle the dispute."

Years passed, and no one rang the bell. Perhaps just seeing the bell in the square caused the citizens to deal fairly with each other. The rope of the bell hung to the ground; over time, a grape vine twined around it.

During those years, a knight returned to Atri from foreign wars. He rode into town on his strong and beautiful horse. He told everyone of the battles. "The only reason I am alive is because this swift steed carried me safely out of danger. I will be grateful all of her days," he told the people.

The knight returned to his farm and put away his sword and armor. He put his beloved horse in a warm stall. "I promise you, my brave friend, you will always have a bed and a bucket of oats." But the horse had been exhausted and chilled in the battles and began to decline in health. At first, the knight took tender care of his animal.

Slowly, the knight forgot about his battles; he became just a busy farmer tending his stock and tilling the soil. The once brave and beautiful horse was now deaf and blind. "You eat too much and you take up too much space," the master said. Finally, one day, he said, "You are useless." He felt justified in taking the old horse out of the stable, taking off her bridle, and driving her off with a stick.

The old horse was confused. She stood outside the gate with her head hung down. Night fell and the wind and snow came. The horse began to stumble around to find shelter and food. In her blind search, she walked toward town. By dawn, the horse was standing in the village square. She chanced upon the rope of the bell which hung to the ground. She began to nibble on the vine encircling the rope. The bell began to ring.

The people poured into the street. "Who calls for justice?" they asked. Everyone knew the knight's horse. They saw her; thin, blind and covered with snow. But they remembered her hour of glory when her master had promised gratitude. "She has a right to ring the bell and demand justice," the people agreed.

The knight was called before the town to explain his cruel behavior; he had no explanation. He was ordered to take care of his horse and treat her with loving kindness for all of her days. The faithful horse was led home to a warm stall and a bucket of oats.

III

There is also a body of stories in which an old man or woman tries to outwit Death, as if that is all old age has to look forward to: the period at the end of a long sentence. But in fact these stories come out of a larger tale tradition—that of the trickster stories, or stories of clever bargainers. These stories remind us that the closer one comes to the end, the sweeter the small victories.

THE OLD MAN AND DEATH

An Old Man had traveled a long and weary road with a heavy bundle of sticks on his back. He found himself so tired, he cast the bundle down and called upon Death to deliver him from his miserable existence.

Straightway Death arrived, his bones clanking and his great scythe sharp and shining in the sun. "You called?"

The Old Man looked once and said quickly, "Pray, good sir, do me the favor of helping me up with my burden again."

For [says Aesop] it is one thing to call for Death, it is quite another to see him coming.

So Death is—if not defeated, at least put off. Or swindled. For a while.

Perhaps that is because as one ages, Death is seen as a Companion, or at least a nodding acquaintance—someone one can negotiate with.

"The reports of my death," Mark Twain once wrote, "have been grossly exaggerated." And so it is with these gray heroes.

Similarly, there are stories in which the old person outwits a doctor, Death's right-hand man. In this Yiddish story, the tart *yenta* has the last word.

IRON LOGIC

An old Jewish woman, just turned ninety, became ill and called the doctor. He examined her carefully and looked doubtful.

"Can you cure me, doctor?" the old woman asked, hopefully.

"Dear Granny," said the doctor, soothingly, "you know what happens when one gets older. All sorts of ailments begin to happen. After all, a doctor is not a miracle man. He cannot make an old woman younger."

"Who's asking you to make me younger, doctor?" protested the old woman irritably. "What I want is to grow older!"

The picture of a drooling, trembling, tart-mouthed, complaining old person is not a pretty one. In fact, in a great many folktales, the old person is considered crafty, whining, wily, scheming—a witch or a miser, a nag or a conniver. If this were the only way the elderly could be found in folktales, the story tradition would be very poor indeed. It takes quite a bit of searching to find the tales in which the elderly are treated with respect, even awe. But the stories are there—just buried under a dusty tarpaulin.

Of course, there is also a group of tales in which Death, or the Spirit of Old Age, does the outwitting. From Japan comes this little gem.

ONE MORE GIFT

On New Year's Eve, the god of Age gives a year to each person.

A round rice cake which is called "Otoshidama" (Year End Gift) stands for age.

An old woman in one village decided that she wanted no

more years because she was old enough. On that evening, she hid
herself in a hole under a pile of rice straw.

The god of Age came to the pile and said,

"Oh, how are you, old woman? This gift is meant for you.
There is another year to spare. I'll give it to you, too."

The old woman, who didn't want any more years, got two
at one time.

IV

Muriel Rukeyser has a poem about an old woman who tells
the reader:

> *"Tickle me up*
> *I'll be*
> *dead very soon—*
> *Nothing will*
> *touch me then. . . ."*

It is that race with the end of life that informs the best of
the folktales about the elderly, infusing them with a zest and
wisdom and power. The old people in these stories may
know they have only a few miles to go before they sleep. Yet,
all undaunted, they do what must be done. These are stories
about those last bits of "tickling up."

Where is meaning to be found in these stories? They can
be reread from Freudian or Jungian perspectives. They can offer up cartloads of interpretations, though I tend to believe
with Marie Louise Van Franz that "the fairy tale itself is its

own best explanation; that is, its meaning is contained in the totality of its motifs connected by the thread of story."

What the folk stories do is to give us a narrative—often rife with familiar images or themes or adages—that play out enormous possibilities. An active, engaged, and powerful old age is one such possibility. The tales explicate in story the old anecdote about Margaret Fuller who—throwing her arms wide—exclaimed, "I accept the universe." To which Ralph Waldo Emerson retorted cynically, "Madam, you damn well better!"

The following Eskimo story encapsulates that active engagement.

THE TWO FRIENDS WHO SET OFF
TO TRAVEL ROUND THE WORLD

Once there were two men who desired to travel round the world, that they might tell others what was the manner of it.

This was in the days when men were still many on the earth, and there were people in all the lands. Now we grow fewer and fewer. Evil and sickness have come upon men. See how I, who tell this story, drag my life along, unable to stand upon my feet.

The two men who were setting out had each newly taken a wife, and had as yet no children. They made themselves cups of musk-ox horn, each making a cup for himself from one side of the same beast's head. And they set out, each going away from the other, that they might go by different ways and meet again some day. They travelled with sledges, and chose land to stay and live upon each summer.

It took them a long time to get round the world; they had

children, and they grew old, and then their children also grew old,
until at last the parents were so old that they could not walk, but
the children led them.

And at last one day, they met—and of their drinking horns
there was but the handle left, so many times had they drunk wa-
ter by the way, scraping the horn against the ground as they filled
them.

"The world is great indeed," they said when they met.

They had been young at their starting, and now they were
old men, led by their children.

Truly the world is great.

V

No one who is over 45 passes by a mirror easily. We are constantly amazed at the elderly person we see reflected back.
The simple fact of aging always seems to surprise us; inside
we do not feel such monumental changes.

As a 105-year-old of my acquaintance once remarked
with a small twist of her mouth, "I cannot believe I have an
eighty-year-old son!"

Yet the gray heroes in folktales do not often wrestle with
such problems. Perhaps it is because we catch them in the
middle of an adventure. They simply do not have time within
their stories to think about what we now like to call "the aging process."

There is a category of stories in the folk culture that is
concerned with the ages of humanity, the span of life. It is
Tale Type 828: "Men and Animals Readjust Span of Life."

But the old person in this story is no hero. He or she is simply a receiver of the gift of a long life, a gift (the story is quick to recognize) which is not necessarily a good or a welcome one.

This is an Israeli version.

THE SPAN OF MAN'S LIFE

When the Holy One created Adam, he showed him the beauty of the world and said, "You will rule over all you see, and you will be very happy."

"How long will I be able to enjoy all this goodness?" enquired Adam.

"Thirty years," was the answer.

"Such a short time?" asked Adam in surprise. "Could you not add a few extra years?"

So God took those extra years from the donkey, the dog, and the monkey.

The first period is until the age of thirty, when a man enjoys the years of his own life to the full and is strong, independent, and carefree.

In the second period, from thirty to fifty years, he is usually married and a father. He has the burden of earning a living and providing for his family. To satisfy his children's and wife's needs, he works like a donkey. These are the twenty years of a donkey's life.

In the third period, from fifty to seventy years, a man serves his children and guards their property as a faithful dog. Usually he does not eat at his children's table. These are the twenty years of a dog's life.

Then comes the last period, from the age of seventy to one hundred. In that period, man loses his teeth, his face becomes wrinkled, and his way of walking and his movements are strange. His children laugh and make fun of him, and it is as if he had departed from this life. These are the thirty years of a monkey's life.

Of course, the obsession with staying young or finding a single pill to keep the aging process at bay is not new. Ponce de León looked for the Fountain of Youth which—so it was claimed—existed somewhere in Florida. But well before that legend took hold, wizards, magi, and charlatans of every stripe promised those who could pay them well a variety of charms that would make them young. In the Middle Ages the blood of boys was transfused into old men, because it was thought that would rejuvenate them. Ancient Persians sliced up snakes believing that the parts would crawl to a special herb which would make it whole again. Once found, the herb was to be swallowed by the magician and a charm spoken. Done properly, this was supposed to confer life everlasting.

Gerontologists, of course, agree that there is no realistic charm (read: medication, herb, hormone, therapy, exercise, new belief systems) to solve all the problems of aging. Still, a recent American Association of Retired Persons Bulletin warns that "Americans spend billions annually on books, supplements, cosmetics, and surgery aimed at staying young."

We have no charm yet, but each year we also move forward in our knowledge about stretching the elastic age band. For example, about 125,000 Americans now get hip replacements each year, and 240,000 get new knees. In the past fifteen years joint replacement has become both safe and effective, and a great majority of the patients are elderly.

Could it be possible that we will eventually learn how to prolong life indefinitely? And even if such a thing is feasible, is it desirable? That is the stuff of science fiction, surely?

But occasionally a folktale has already wrestled succinctly with the same question. This Chinese story from 1,600 years ago is a perfect example.

THE MORTAL LORD

The patriarch Ching of the land of Ch'i was with his companions on Mount Ox. As he looked northward out over his capital, tears rose in his eyes. "Such a splendid land," he said, "swarming, burgeoning; if only I didn't have to die and leave it as the waters pass! What if from the eldest times there were no death: would I ever have to leave here?"

His companions joined him in weeping. "Even for the simple fare we eat," they said, "for the nag and plank wagon we have to ride, we depend upon our lord's generosity. If we have no wish to die, how much less must our lord."

Yen Tzu was the only one smiling, somewhat apart. The patriarch wiped away his tears and looked hard at Yen Tzu. "These two who weep with me share the sadness I feel on today's venture," said the patriarch. "Why do you alone smile, sir?"

"What if the worthiest ruled forever?" asked Yen Tzu. "Then T'ai or Huan would be patriarch forever. What if the bravest? Then Chuang or Ling would be patriarch forever. With such as those in power, my lord, you would now be in the rice fields wearing a straw cape and bamboo hat, careworn from dig-

ging, with no time to brood over death. And then, my lord, how
could you have reached the position you now hold? It was through
the succession of your predecessors, who held and vacated the
throne each in his turn, that you came to be lord over this land.
For you alone to lament this is selfish. Seeing a selfish lord and
his fawning, flattering subjects, I presumed to smile."

The patriarch was embarrassed, raised his flagon, and penal-
ized his companions two drafts of wine apiece.

As the punch line to the old joke about growing older
goes: "Consider the alternative."

The stories in this book do just that. The aged and the
elderly heroes fight dragons, make love, set things aright with
a bit of well-worn wisdom. They save their grandchildren, a
city, a kingdom, a castle, a king. They meet the enemy with
courage and compassion and cunning, when often the young-
sters around them have neither.

These gray heroes do not have "senior moments," those
instants when memory fails. They do not fish for names or
nouns. While they do not disguise the fact that they are old,
they are not simply Yeats's "tattered coat upon a stick."

They wear their long years well.

NOW I BECOME MYSELF

Now I become myself. It's taken
Time, many years and places;
I have been dissolved and shaken,
Worn other people's faces,
Run madly, as if Time were there,

Terribly old, crying a warning,
"Hurry, you will be dead before——"
(What? Before you reach the morning?
Or the end of the poem is clear?
Or love safe in the walled city?)
Now to stand still, to be here,
Feel my own weight and density!
The black shadow on the paper
Is my hand; the shadow of a word
As thought shapes the shaper
Falls heavy on the page, is heard.
All fuses now, falls into place
From wish to action, word to silence,
My work, my love, my time, my face
Gathered into one intense
Gesture of growing like a plant.
As slowly as the ripening fruit
Fertile, detached, and always spent,
Falls but does not exhaust the root,
So all the poem is, can give,
Grows in me to become the song;
Made so and rooted so by love.
Now there is time and Time is young.
O, in this single hour I live
All of myself and do not move.
I, the pursued, who madly ran,
Stand still, stand still, and stop the sun!

—MAY SARTON

Gray Heroes

Wisdom

The most popular positive
characterization of an old person in
folklore is that of the wise man or
wise woman, the sage, the magic
helper. There is often an androgyny of
character in these stories and, indeed,
the same role is played as often by
men as by women regardless of
country or culture or tribe.

The wise man is characterized as
the sage, the seer, the speaker of
otherwise unutterable truths. He
carries a culture on his old shoulders.
He reminds us of what we should
already know by reason, and he tells us
what we might not otherwise know
about the gods, the seasons, the ways
of planting, and life itself.

The wise woman is seen as the crone, the dark and waning moon, the hag, the keeper of the mysteries: of birth, of death, of the growing corn, and of the changing tides.

Job asks, "But where shall wisdom be found?"

Surely one of the answers is: In the great body of story.

An Old Man and a Boy

A long time ago, there was a land called "Wells," because it had a lot of water wells. People and animals drank water from the wells. But, during the dry season, the water level was always low because of lack of rains.

One day, an old man found a boy sitting next to a well and asked him, "What are you waiting for while sitting next to the well?"

The boy answered, "I am waiting for the well to be full of water so that I can drink from it."

The old man then told him, "Child, if you don't kneel down to drink, you will only drink when the rains come."

Empty-Cup Mind

JAPAN

A wise old monk once lived in an ancient temple in Japan. One day the monk heard an impatient pounding on the temple door. He opened it and greeted a young student, who said, "I have studied with great and wise masters. I consider myself quite accomplished in Zen philosophy. However, just in case there is anything more I need to know, I have come to see if you can add to my knowledge."

"Very well," said the wise old master. "Come and have tea with me, and we will discuss your studies." The two seated themselves opposite each other, and the old monk prepared tea. When it was ready, the old monk began to pour the tea carefully into the visitor's cup. When the cup was full, the old man continued pouring until the tea spilled over the side of the cup and onto the young man's lap. The startled visitor jumped back and indignantly shouted, "Some wise master you are! You are a fool who does not even know when a cup is full!"

The old man calmly replied, "Just like this cup, your mind is so full of ideas that there is no room for any more. Come to me with an empty-cup mind, and then you will learn something."

The Old Woman of the Spring

NATIVE AMERICAN/CHEYENNE

When the Cheyenne were still in the north, they camped in a large circle at whose entrance a deep, rapid spring flowed from a hillside. The spring provided the camp with water, but food was harder to find. The buffalo had disappeared, and many people went hungry.

One bright day some men were playing the game of ring

and javelin in the center of the camp circle. They used a red and black hoop and four long sticks, two red and two black, which they threw at the hoop as it rolled along. In order to win, a player had to throw his stick through the hoop while it was still moving.

A large audience had already gathered when a young man came from the south side of the camp circle to join them. He wore a buffalo robe with the hair turned outward. His body was painted yellow, and a yellow-painted eagle breech-feather was fastened to his head. Soon another young man dressed exactly like the first came from the north side of the circle to watch the game. They were unacquainted, but when the two caught sight of each other they moved through the crowd to talk. "My friend," said the man from the south side, "you're imitating my dress. Why are you doing it?" The other man said, "It's you who are imitating me. Why?"

In their explanations, both men told the same story. They had entered the spring that flowed out from the hillside, and there they had been instructed how to dress. By now the crowd had stopped watching the game and gathered around to listen, and the young men told the people that they would go into the spring again and come out soon. As the crowd watched, the two approached the spring. The man from the south covered his head with his buffalo robe and entered. The other did the same.

The young men splashed through the water and soon found themselves in a large cave. Near the entrance sat an old woman cooking some buffalo meat and corn in two separate earthen pots. She welcomed them: "Grandchildren, you have come. Here, sit beside me." They sat down, one on each side of her, and told her that the people were hungry and that they had come to her for food. She gave them corn from one pot and meat from the other. They ate until they had had enough, and when they were through the pots were still full. Then she told them to look toward the south, and they saw that the land in that direction was covered with buffalo. She told them to look to the west, and they saw all kinds of animals, large and small, including ponies, though they knew nothing of ponies in those days. She told them to look toward the north, and they saw corn growing everywhere.

The old woman said to them, "All this that you have seen shall be yours in the future. Tonight I cause the buffalo to be restored to you. When you leave this place, the buffalo will follow, and your people will see them coming before sunset. Take this uncooked corn in your robes, and plant it every spring in low, moist ground. After it matures, you can feed upon it.

"Take also this meat and corn that I have cooked," she said, "and when you have returned to your people, ask them to sit down to eat in the following order: First, all males, from the youngest to the oldest, with the exception of one orphan boy; second, all females, from the oldest to the youngest, with the exception of one orphan girl. When all are through eating, the rest of the food in the pots is to be eaten by the orphan boy and the orphan girl."

The two men obeyed the old woman. When they passed out of the spring, they saw that their entire bodies were painted red, and the yellow breech-feathers on their heads had turned red. They went to their people, who ate as directed of the corn and meat. There was enough for all, and the contents of the pots remained full until they were passed to the two orphan children, who ate all the rest of the food.

Toward sunset the people went to their lodges and began watching the spring closely, and in a short time they saw a buffalo leap out. The creature jumped and played and rolled, then returned to the spring. In a little while another buffalo jumped out, then another and another, and finally they came so fast that the Cheyenne were no longer able to count them. The buffalo continued to emerge all night, and the following day the whole country out in the distance was covered with buffalo. The buffalo scented the great camp. The next day the Cheyenne surrounded them, for though the men hunted on foot, they ran very fast.

For a time the people had an abundance of buffalo meat. In the spring they moved their camp to low, swampy land, where they planted the corn they had received from the medicine stream. It grew rapidly, and every grain they planted brought forth strong stalks bearing two to four ears of corn. The people planted corn every year after this.

One spring after planting corn, the Cheyenne went on a buffalo hunt. When they had enough meat to last for a long time, they returned to their fields. To their surprise, they found that the corn had been stolen by some neighboring tribe. Nothing but stalks remained—not even a kernel for seed. Though the theft had occurred about a moon before, the Cheyenne trailed the enemy's footprints for several days. They even fought with two or three tribes, but never succeeded in tracing the robbers or recovering the stolen crop. It was a long time before the Cheyenne planted any more corn.

The Brownie of Blednock

SCOTLAND

Did you ever hear how a Brownie came to our village of Blednock, and was frightened away again by a silly young wife, who thought she was cleverer than anyone else, but who did us the worst turn that she ever did anybody in her life, when she made the queer, funny, useful little man disappear?

Well, it was one November evening, in the gloaming, just when the milking was done, and before the bairns were put to bed, and everyone was standing on their doorsteps, having a crack about the bad harvest, and the turnips, and what chances there were of good prices for the bullocks at the Martinmas Fair, when the queerest humming noise started down by the river.

It came nearer and nearer, and everyone stopped their gossip and began to look down the road. And, deed, it was no wonder that they stared, for there, coming up the middle of the highway, was the strangest, most frightsome-looking creature that human eyes had ever seen.

He looked like a little wee, wee man, and yet he looked like a beast, for he was covered with hair from head to foot, and he wore no clothing except a little kilt of green rushes which hung round his waist. His hair was matted, and his head hung forward on his breast, and he had a long blue beard, which almost touched the ground.

His legs were twisted, and knocked together as he walked,

and his arms were so long that his hands trailed in the mud.

He seemed to be humming something over and over again, and as he came near us we could just make out the words, "Hae ye wark for Aiken-Drum?"

Eh, but I can tell you the folk were scared. If it had been the Evil One himself who had come to our quiet little village, I doubt if he would have caused more stir. The bairns screamed, and hid their faces in their mothers' gown-tails, while the lassies, idle huzzies that they were, threw down the pails of milk, which should have been in the milkhouse long ago, if they had not been so busy gossiping; and the very dogs crept in behind their masters, whining, and hiding their tails between their legs. The grown men, who should have known better, and who were not frightened to look the wee man in the face, laughed and hooted at him.

"Did ye ever see such eyes?" cried one.

"His mouth is so big, he could swallow the moon," said another.

"Hech, sirs, but did ye ever see such a creature?" cried the third.

And still the poor little man went slowly up the street, crying wistfully, "Hae ye wark for Aiken-Drum? Any wark for Aiken-Drum?"

Some of us tried to speak to him, but our tongues seemed to be tied, and the words died away on our lips, and we could only stand and watch him with frightened glances, as if we were bewitched.

Old Grannie Duncan, the oldest, and the kindest woman in the village, was the first to come to her senses. "He may be a ghost, or a bogle, or a wraith," she said; "or he may only be a harmless Brownie. It is beyond me to say; but this I know that if he be an evil spirit, he will not dare to look on the Holy Book." And with that she ran into her cottage, and brought out the great leather-bound Bible which aye lay on her little table by the window.

She stood on the road, and held it out, right in front of the creature, but he took no more heed of it than if it had been an old song-book, and went slowly on, with his weary cry for work.

"He's just a Brownie," cried Grannie Duncan in triumph, "a simple, kindly Brownie. I've heard tell of such folk before, and many a long day's work will they do for the people who treat them well."

Gathering courage from her words, we all crowded round the wee man, and now that we were close to him, we saw that his hairy face was kind and gentle and his tiny eyes had a merry twinkle in them.

"Save us, and help us, creature!" said an old man reprovingly, "but can ye no speak, and tell us what ye want, and where ye come from?"

For answer the Brownie looked all round him, and gave such a groan, that we scattered and ran in all directions, and it was full five minutes before we could pluck up our courage and go close to him again.

But Grannie Duncan stood her ground, like a brave old woman that she was, and it was to her that the creature spoke.

"I cannot tell thee from whence I come," he said. " 'Tis a nameless land, and 'tis very different from this land of thine. For there we all learn to serve, while here everyone wishes to be served. And when there is no work for us to do at home, then we sometimes set out to visit thy land, to see if there is any work which we may do there. I must seem strange to human eyes, that I know; but if thou wilt, I will stay in this place awhile. I need not that any should wait on me, for I seek neither wages, nor clothes, nor bedding. All I ask for is the corner of a barn to sleep in, and a cogful of brose set down on the floor at bedtime; and if no one meddles with me, I will be ready to help anyone who needs me. I'll gather your sheep betimes on the hill; I'll take in your harvest by moonlight. I'll sing the bairns to sleep in their cradles, and, though I doubt you'll not believe it, you'll find that the babes will love me. I'll kirn your kirns for you, goodwives, and I'll bake your bread on a busy day; while, as for the men folk, they may find me useful when there is corn to thrash, or untamed colts in the stable, or when the waters are out in flood."

No one quite knew what to say to answer to the creature's strange request. It was an unheard-of thing for anyone to come and offer their services for nothing, and the men began to whisper among themselves, and to say that it was not canny, and 'twere better to have nothing to do with him.

But up spoke Old Grannie Duncan again. " 'Tis but a Brownie, I tell you," she repeated, "a poor, harmless Brownie, and many a story have I heard in my young days about the work that a Brownie can do, if he be well treated and let alone. Have we not been complaining all summer about bad times, and scant wages, and a lack of workmen to work the work? And now, when a workman comes ready to your hand, ye will have none of him, just because he is not bonnie to look on."

Still the men hesitated, and the silly young wenches screwed their faces, and pulled their mouths. "But, Grannie," cried they, "that is all very well, but if we keep such a creature in our village, no one will come near it, and then what shall we do for sweethearts?"

"Shame on ye," cried Grannie impatiently, "and on all you men for encouraging the silly things in their whimsies. It's time that ye were thinking o' other things than bonnie faces and sweethearts. 'Handsome is that handsome does,' is a good old saying; and what about the corn that stands rotting in the fields, an' it past Hallowe'en already? I've heard that a Brownie can stack a whole ten-acre field in a single night."

That settled the matter. The miller offered the creature the corner of his barn to sleep in, and Grannie promised to boil the cogful of brose, and send her grandchild, wee Jeannie, down with it every evening, and then we all said goodnight, and went into our houses, looking over our shoulders as we did so, for fear that the strange little man was following us.

But if we were afraid of him that night, we had a very different song to sing before a week was over. Whatever he was, or whatever he came from, he was the most wonderful worker that men had ever known. And the strange thing was that he did most of it at night. He had the corn safe into the stackyards and the stacks thatched, in the clap of a hand, as the old folk say.

The village became the talk of the countryside, and folk came from all parts to see if they could catch a glimpse of our queer, hairy little visitor; but they were always unsuccessful, for he was never to be seen when one looked for him. One might go into the miller's barn twenty times a day, and twenty times a day find nothing but a heap of straw; and although the cog of brose was aye empty in the morning, no one knew when he came home, or when he supped it.

But wherever there was work to be done, whether it was a sickly bairn to be sung to, or a house to be tidied up; a kirn that would not kirn, or a batch of bread that would not rise; a flock of sheep to be gathered together on a stormy night, or a bundle to be carried home by some weary labourer, Aiken-Drum, as we learned to call him, always got to know of it, and appeared in the nick of time. It looked as if we had all got wishing-caps, for we had just to wish, and the work was done.

Many a time, some poor mother, who had been up with a crying babe all night, would sit down with it in her lap, in front of the fire, in the morning, and fall fast asleep, and when she awoke, she would find that Aiken-Drum had paid her a visit, for the floor would be washed, and the dishes too, and the fire made up, and the kettle put on to boil; but the little man would have slipped away, as if he were frightened of being thanked.

The bairns were the only ones who ever saw him idle, and oh, how they loved him! In the gloaming, or when the school was out, one could see them away down in some corner by the burn-side, crowding round the little dark brown figure, with its kilt of rushes, and one would hear the sound of wondrous low sweet singing, for he knew all the songs that the little ones loved.

So by and by the name of Aiken-Drum came to be a household word amongst us, and although we so seldom saw him near at hand, we loved him like one of our ain folk.

And he might have been here still, had it not been for a silly, senseless young wife who thought she knew better than everyone else, and who took some idle notion into her empty head that it was not right to make the little man work, and give him no wage.

She dinned this into our heads, morning, noon, and night, and she would not believe us when we told her that Aiken-Drum worked for love, and love only.

Poor thing, she could not understand anyone doing that, so she made up her mind that she, at least, would do what was right, and set us all an example.

She did not mean any harm, she said afterwards, when the miller took her to task for it; but although she might not mean to do any harm, she did plenty, as senseless folk are apt to do when they cannot bear to take other people's advice, for she took a pair of her husband's old, mouldy, worn-out breeches, and laid them down one night beside the cogful of brose.

By my faith, if the village folk had not remembered so well what Aiken-Drum had said about wanting no wages, they would have found something better to give him than a pair of worn-out breeks.

Be that as it may, the long and the short of it was, that the dear wee man's feelings were hurt because we would not take his services for nothing, and he vanished in the night, as Brownies are apt to do, so Grannie Duncan says, if anyone

tries to pay them, and we have never seen him from that day
to this, although the bairns declare that they sometimes hear
him singing down by the mill, as they pass it in the gloaming,
on their way home from school.

The Wise Woman

ALGERIA

The people of a village in Algeria were under siege. Lack of
food, water, and medical supplies had nearly reduced them to
total destruction. Many had already died, and the remaining
few were losing hope.

The mayor called a meeting and said, "My dear friends,
the end is near. If we don't surrender immediately we will all
die anyway. Perhaps our enemy will take pity on those of us
who are still alive if we submit to them now."

The villagers listened with heavy hearts, bowing their
heads with this latest burden. Then Aicha came forward. She
was an ancient woman, but her eyes were still bright and she
walked with dignity.

She turned to the people. "We must not give in just yet. I
have an idea and if you will help me I believe we will be
saved."

"What is your plan, Aicha?" the major asked.

"First I will need a calf!" said Aicha firmly.

The mayor was dismayed. "How can you request a calf? There has not been a calf in our village for months."

But Aicha insisted she needed a calf, and the villagers searched far and wide for one. And after some time they found a calf in the shed of a stingy old man who had hoped to sell it later for a healthy price. The villagers triumphantly brought the calf to Aicha, leaving the old man sputtering in anger at his loss.

"You have done well," praised Aicha when she saw the calf. "Now bring me some corn."

The villagers groaned upon hearing her request. But she entreated them to search everywhere. And soon they all returned with bits and pieces of corn until there was enough to fill a bucket. Aicha added some water to it and fed it to the calf.

"How can you feed that calf when children are crying for a bit to eat and people are dying of hunger each day?" asked the mayor.

But Aicha continued to feed the calf, stating, "Have faith, sir, and you will see that this will save our village."

The mayor resigned himself to giving in to her. When the calf had finished eating, Aicha led it to the city wall and told the sentry to open the gates. The mayor had followed and nodded to the sentry to do as she requested. When the gates were opened Aicha pushed out the calf which began to graze on the grass outside the gates.

The enemy was watching and wasted no time in capturing the cow and taking it in triumph to their leaders. The enemy king was stunned when he saw what they had brought.

"How can this be?" exclaimed the king. "I thought the

villagers were starving and yet they have a calf that they can spare. They must be better prepared than we had assumed. However, let us not waste it. We shall feast tonight."

The men soon had slaughtered the cow and were shocked to find that the cow's stomach contained undigested corn. They took this news to the king, who became even more concerned.

"If these villagers can feed corn to this calf they must have more food than we do. We cannot outlast them or we will be the ones who starve." The king's men agreed and the king gave the order to retreat.

The next morning the sentry ran to the mayor with the grand news. The mayor gathered the villagers and announced that as Aicha had promised, the enemy had departed. The villagers cheered Aicha and she lived the remainder of her days with honor and comfort.

An Old Man Who Saved
Some Ungrateful People

ZIMBABWE

In a certain village there lived people who were both happy and rich. They had very good fields there, and each year they harvested so much grain that their grain bins were full to overflowing. Some of the grain bins were so full, in fact, that the tree trunks which served as their legs broke and tipped the bins to the ground. This did not matter, as there was far more grain than was needed.

The birds heard about this village and decided that it would be a good place for birds to live. They arrived one morning, in a great fluttering cloud, and settled themselves on trees around the fields. Then, when the people had finished their work in the fields, the birds flew down and ate as much grain as they could manage. Then they flew back to their places in the trees and slept until the next morning.

The people were worried when they saw the next morning how much of the grain had been eaten by these greedy birds. They shouted at the trees and shook their fists, but the birds just sang and paid no attention to the people below them.

The people returned to the village and got out all their bows and arrows. Then they walked back to the fields and aimed the arrows at the birds.

It was easy for the birds to avoid the arrows. As they saw them coming through the air, they just flew up until the arrows had passed. Then they landed on their branches again and began to sing.

"We shall soon starve," the women said to the headman. "If you do nothing, all the people in this village will stop being fat and will become very thin."

The headman knew that what they said was right. And yet he could think of no way in which they could deal with the birds. If their arrows did not work, then there was no other weapon at their disposal.

They talked and talked about the problem until one of the young men said:

"There is always that old man—the one we all chased away from the village. He knows many magic things and may be able to do something about the birds."

Everybody was silent. They had all been thinking the same thing but nobody had been courageous enough to talk about it. The old man had been chased away because of his spells and now they were going to have to beg him to come back again.

"Where does he live now?" asked the headman. "I think we shall have to go and speak to him."

The young man explained that he had seen the old man living in a bush not far away. He would be able to take the headman there and show him the place.

When the headman arrived at the bush in which the old man lived, he was saddened to see him in such a state. All his clothes were now rags and his cheeks were hollow. There were few leaves left on the bush, as the old man had been forced to eat leaves to deal with the great hunger which plagued him.

The headman greeted the old man and said how sorry he was that he had not seen him for such a long time. The old man looked at him, but said nothing.

"We are having a problem with birds," the headman then said. "Although we have good crops, the birds come down from the trees and eat all our grain. Soon we will be as poor as you are."

"You should shoot the birds," the old man said. "That's how you solve that problem."

"These birds are too clever," the headman said. "When our arrows come close to them, they hop up in the air and are unharmed."

The old man thought for a moment before he spoke again.

"I cannot help you," he said. "You made me leave that place before, and now I'm living in this new place."

The headman had feared that the old man would say something like this. He begged him to think again, and when the old man still said no, he begged him again. At last the old man agreed to come, although he was unhappy to leave the bush in which he was living.

Before they returned to the village, the old man went to a number of secret places which he knew and collected roots and other substances that he would need for his work. Then they went back to the village, where all the people were waiting to welcome the old man back into their midst.

The next morning, the old man called everybody in the village to the door of his hut. From a pouch which he had with him, he took out powders which he had made from the roots and other substances. Everybody was then told to dip the tips of their arrows into this powder and, when they had done this, to go down to the fields and wait for him to come.

The birds watched the people gathering at the edge of the fields and laughed amongst themselves. The leader of the birds fluffed up his feathers and began to sing a special bird song which was all about how birds enjoyed eating the food of foolish people. Just as he sang, the old man took an arrow from a young man's bow and shot it towards the singing bird. The bird rose into the air, laughing at the useless weapons of the people below, but the arrow followed him upwards and pierced the centre of his heart.

All the other birds were silent when they saw what had happened to their leader. Before they could rise from their branches, though, many other arrows came up through the air and struck them down. After a few minutes, there were very few birds left, and these few took wing for the hills.

The village people were so happy at the fact that they had been saved that they took the old man to the largest hut they had and made him their new chief. They gave him four cows and a great supply of beer. Whenever he needed anything, he had only to ask, and it would be delivered to him.

The old man was happy to be a chief, and he ruled well. He never made unfair decisions, and he never took more than his fair share of anything. When people were squabbling over some little matter, he would settle the argument wisely. Everybody was content at the way he ruled.

After a while, some people began to talk about how the old man must still have powers to work magic.

"If he did it before," they said, "then he might do it again. He knows how these powders work."

Other people agreed.

"Perhaps one day he might use his magic against us," one man said. "If he did that, we would be powerless to stop him."

"We would be like the birds," another said. "He could shoot an arrow into our heart."

Such talk was soon going all around the village. Eventually when enough people had heard it, they gathered in a crowd outside the old man's hut and shouted out for him to leave. The old man looked out of his door and was surprised to see the people standing there.

"I have done no wrong," he said. "Why are you asking me to leave?"

"Because you are too clever," the people said. "We are frightened of you."

The old man went back into his hut but soon came out again. Carrying the pouch with his powders in it, he left the village and returned to the bush where he had been living before he became chief. Satisfied with their work, the people had a party the next day to celebrate the departure of the old man. They did not see the birds sitting on the branches, watching the party.

When the people saw that the birds had returned, they began to wail.

"We shall have to find the old man again," they said. "We must bring him back to the village or we shall again lose all our crops."

As the birds descended on the fields and began to eat the grain, four of the most important men from the village ran off to find the old man. It took them some time to find him, but at last they reached the bush where he lived.

"You must come back to the village," they said. "We shall give you back your hut and your cows. You must come back."

The old man looked at the ungrateful people who stood before him. Then he looked at the bush, with its few leaves and the hard ground around it.

"No," he said.

An Old Man's Wisdom

INDIA

Once upon a time, in a certain village, an old man advised other men to spend their time cultivating rice. But those others went right along hunting wild animals and fishing in the streams. They gathered wild yams and wild fruits, not heeding the old man in the least. The work in the fields was entrusted to women, while the men kept on roaming the forest in search of wild foods. Soon the crops were overgrown with weeds, because the work of women alone was not enough to keep back the jungle.

The old man had a grandson who was very smart. Indeed the two lived together in the same house. The boy wanted to follow his friends hunting and fishing in the forest. He asked his grandfather's permission to go, but the senior man always refused. Grandfather was still strong and healthy, and he worked diligently in his fields. Still he insisted that his grandson come with him, and that they work together the whole day, every day, from planting right up to harvest time.

One day the grandson asked his grandfather if he might go with the other boys to hunt and fish in the forest. The old man gently denied his request. Instead, he asked that his grandson's friend bring back a small fish, alive. The friend agreed. Later that day he returned with such a fish. The old man then told his grandson to put the fish into the wooden trough often used for feeding pigs.

"Now, boy," said the old man, "catch this fish and give it to me." At first the boy thought it would be easy, so he used only one hand. Not being able to catch it with one, he soon tried with both hands. Still he couldn't catch the fish. Indeed he tried and tried, but he still couldn't succeed. The grandfather, watching him, then said, "Dear grandson, if you cannot catch a fish in a wooden trough at home, how do you expect to catch one in the running water of a stream?" The boy remained silent. The wise old man then told his grandson, "Let us tend to our rice cultivation with full attention. If we have enough rain we will have everything we need. Fish, venison, and meats of all kind will come to us for the asking. You will know more about this magic at harvest time."

Finally the harvest came and the old man and his grandson had an abundance of rice. Two large granaries were filled. But in the fields of others weeds had choked out the rice and the harvest was poor. Most people had barely enough to last for a few months after harvest. The days passed. The other villagers, after finishing their little stock of rice, came to the old man and his grandson to borrow some. They brought with them the fish and game they had hunted in forests. They carried loads of yams and wild fruit they had gathered. All these they gave in exchange for rice, for rice was their staple food and without it they couldn't live.

"I once spoke of the magic by which fish and meat and fruit would come to us at our command. Do you see my reasoning now?" the grandfather asked. "When we have an abundance of rice everything else follows naturally." The boy soon realized the truth of the old man's advice and gave his complete attention to rice cultivation. The other villagers, after several years of famine, followed suit. Thereafter, with hard work, there was always abundance.

Hide Anger Until Tomorrow

SURINAME

There was a man who had to go off to town to work. In town he met this old man who was wise in all things, and who said to him, "I am going to tell you the two things you need to know: When you get angry, hide it until tomorrow; and all that your eyes see, you must not believe."

Now, this man had a wife at home, but they had no child. He had to remain away from home for a long time, but finally he was able to return. But when he came home, he found a man in bed with his wife and they were both asleep. He drew his revolver to shoot the man, but suddenly he remembered what the old man had said to him: "Hide your anger until tomorrow." So he didn't shoot him.

When the morning came and they were all awake, his wife told him of their good luck; for when he left she was pregnant, and this was their boy who was sleeping with his mother. The child had grown so big! If he had shot him, he would have killed his own child.

That is why it is well to listen to a person who says, "Hide your anger till tomorrow, and all that you see you must not believe."

The Three Counsels

MEXICO

Once there was a boy who ran away from home. He had three bad habits: he would not stick to a purpose, he was always inquiring into other people's business, and he would not control his temper. He had hardly gone any distance when he left the highway for a trail, ran into an old man and asked his business, and lost his temper when the man did not reply.

Finally, the *viejito* [little old man] spoke, saying that he was a peddler of advice and for a peso he would tell the boy some. The boy had only three pesos, but he gave one to the old man and was told, "Don't leave a highway for a trail." The boy was angry at such advice, so the viejo said for another peso he would give him more. The second advice was,

"Don't ask about things that don't concern you." Again, the boy was angry, but finally parted with his last peso, only to hear, "Don't lose your temper." And the old man vanished.

The boy went on his way, his pockets empty, and a stranger galloped up on a black horse, advising him to take a shortcut on his road to the city; the boy, however, couldn't stick to a purpose, so he ignored the path. He came to a ranch house, and a bandit seated in front of the house invited him to dinner. When a man's head was served him, he decided that he'd better not ask questions. When the bandit couldn't get any inquiries about the head, he took the boy to see his keepsakes—skeletons of men who were too inquisitive about the head they were served. Since the boy had not been nosy, he was given three mules and a horse, each mule having two bags of gold tied on its back.

As he went down the road with his riches, he came to another bandit who demanded to know what was in the sacks. Instead of losing his temper, the boy said simply that he preferred not to tell. "Speak or I shall kill you," said the bandit. The boy said, "If you feel that is best, then follow your conscience." The bandit, pleased with the boy's wisdom, let him pass.

Soon the boy had gone into business in the city and was doing well, marrying a wealthy girl. But best of all was the fact that she, too, "did not leave the main road for a path, asked no questions about things that did not pertain to her, and always kept her temper."

The Truth

SYRIA

A king once ordered that whoever told a lie should pay a fine of five dinars. The crier went through the city announcing the command, and people began to avoid each other, fearing that they might speak an untruth. Meanwhile the king and his *wazir* disguised themselves and wandered about the marketplace to see the effects of the decree.

They paused in front of the store of a rich merchant—though who is rich beside Allah? The merchant invited them in and served them coffee, and they passed the time pleasantly in conversation. "How old are you?" they asked. "Twenty," said the merchant. "What are you worth?" "Seventy thousand." "How many children do you have?" "One by the grace of God."

When the king and the *wazir* returned to the palace, they checked the records and sent for the merchant. "How old did you say you were?" "Twenty." "That will cost you five dinars. And how much are you worth?" "Seventy thousand." "That will be another five dinars. And how many sons do you have?" "One, by Allah." "Pay another five dinars." "First prove your case against me," said the merchant. "You are an old man—sixty-five years old, according to the books—and yet you claim you are only twenty!" "The years I enjoyed and in which I found happiness are but twenty—of the rest I know nothing." "Then what about your vast wealth, so large that it cannot be counted or calculated, while you admit to seventy thousand only." "With those seventy thousand I built a mosque. That is my fortune—the money I dedicated to God and man." "Well, do you deny that you have six sons?" they asked, and named them one by one. "No, but five are godless drunkards and adulterers. Only one, may God look kindly on him, is upright and good."

"You have spoken well, O truthful one," the king admitted. "No time is worth remembering but that which was passed in bliss; no wealth worth counting but that spent for the cause of God and man; and no son worth mentioning unless he is pious and good."

The Old Man and the Grain of Wheat

RUSSIA

A king once went hunting in the fall when the grain was golden on the hillsides. As he pursued a deer, he crossed an open field in the center of which, on a flat rock, he found a single grain of wheat as large as a sparrow's egg. The king marveled greatly at what he saw, and, calling his boyars together, asked them if they had ever seen its like before. As none had, he sent for the villagers. They, likewise, were astonished at the size of the grain.

At last one said, "There is a very old man living not far from here who may be able to tell us something."

"Send for him!" commanded the king.

When the old man appeared, he was led by a guide and hobbled along with a crutch under each arm.

"Honored sire," said he, "I have never seen such a grain before, but my father may be able to tell you something."

"Send for him!" commanded the king.

When the old father appeared, he walked by himself, but hobbled along with a cane in one hand and a crutch under his other arm.

"Honored sire," said he, "I have a dim recollection that they grew such grain in the days of my father. Why do you not send for him. He may tell you something."

"Send for him!" commanded the king.

When the old grandfather appeared, he skipped over a stone fence as lively as a goat, made a graceful bow to the king, and said, "Honored sire, I see you have a grain of my wheat in your hand."

"Your wheat?" asked the king.

"Yes," answered the old grandfather. "In the days of my youth I grew such wheat and have, even now, some souvenirs stored in my barn. A mouse must have carried this grain to the spot where you found it."

"That is interesting," said the king. "Now explain to me why the wheat of the present is smaller than the wheat of your day!"

"Because," said the old grandfather, "in my day people worked harder, needed less, and were satisfied with what was good for them."

"A very fine explanation," said the king. "Tell me now how it happens that you, a grandfather, and at least one hundred seventy years of age, should walk with one crutch less than your son, and two less than your grandson?"

"The reason is the same," said the old man. "I worked hard, needed little to keep me well, and was satisfied with what was good for me instead of envying my neighbor and trying to keep up with him. Thus my body remained free from the ills of the flesh and my mind remained free from the ills that attack the souls of those who are selfish."

The king marveled at the words of the old man and gave him a gold piece as a mark of favor.

Elijah and the Poor Man's Wish

JEWISH

Once in a long ago faraway place, there lived a man who was old, blind, penniless, and childless. Even though there were so many troubles in his life, he was able to get by with joy in his heart, for he had the love of a sweet and kind wife. They had so little, but they were rich in the love they shared for each other. And whatever little they had, they would gladly share with others.

One day the man just needed the time and space to think about things. He had never complained, but now he needed to go somewhere and reflect on his life. He made his way down to the riverbank and began to think of all that had happened to him and how things could have been different.

He was lost in thought when suddenly he heard something in the distance. It was the tap, tap, tapping of a cane coming closer and closer. There was the rustling of a long satin cloak. He smelled an aroma that reminded him of scents so sweet, they might have been in the Garden of Eden. And someone came and sat beside him, saying, "Do you know who I am?"

The old man thought of the sounds and the scent. "Are you . . . you must be Elijah the Prophet!"

"Yes, you are right. I am Elijah, and I have been sent here for a very special reason. God has looked here and has seen your suffering. Yet you do not complain; you are still grateful for life, and you and your dear wife share much joy. And, too, you are always ready to share with those less fortunate than yourselves. So I have been sent here to bring you a message. You will be granted a wish! What shall it be? What is it that you want?"

The old man did not move. He stayed very still, very quiet, thinking. What wish could he make? What did he really want? Should he wish for his sight? his youth? money? . . . Dared he wish for a child? Try as he might, he just couldn't make up his mind.

Finally Elijah spoke again. "I can see that this is a difficult decision, one not easily made. So why not think about it for a while? Go home and consider what you will do. And then I will meet you here tomorrow, same time and same place. You can tell me then what you will wish."

Then the old man heard the rustling of the long satin cloak as Elijah rose to go. He heard the tap, tap, tapping of the cane going off into the distance. But the smell, like all of the scents in the Garden of Eden . . . that scent lingered long after. The old man stayed by the river, listening to the water gently flowing by. After a while he slowly made his way back home.

"Wife! Beloved wife! Come and hear of my adventure!" called the old man as he entered their house. And he told his wife the whole story. When he got to the end of his tale, he asked, "So please help me. What one wish can I make?"

"Do not worry, my wonderful husband. All will be for the best. For now, it is time for dinner. Sit down, have some nice soup and good bread. After dinner, we can rest and tell each other stories. Go to sleep tonight and have sweet dreams, and tomorrow we will decide what you should say."

And that is exactly what the loving couple did. The man had the most beautiful dreams all night long; and in the morning, after breakfast, his wife whispered something in his ear.

"Oh, my sweet wife! What a treasure I have in you! That is exactly the right wish. Now, if only I can remember!" Repeating the wish to himself, the old man left his house and made his way slowly back to his place by the river and began to wait. And he waited and waited, listening for the sounds he had heard the day before.

Soon enough, the old man heard it: the tap, tap, tapping of a cane coming closer and closer. There was the rustling of a long satin cloak; and then, finally, there was the smell like every scent in all of the Garden of Eden. And Elijah the Prophet came and sat down next to the old man.

"*Shalom aleichem!*"

"*Aleichem shalom!*"

"Well, so now it is time. I can grant only one wish for you. What will it be?"

What should he wish for? A child? money? his sight? his youth? his health?

The old man hesitated for a moment. He took a deep breath, and he began:

"May God grant that I live . . . to see the day . . . when my child . . . will eat . . . from a golden plate!"

Elijah threw back his head and began to laugh and laugh. "I can see that you have managed to get all of your wishes into one wish! I'll bet that God is enjoying this just as much as I am. And I am certain that God will see to it that every part of your beautiful wish is granted."

For a moment, all was still and silent. Then the old man heard the rustling of the long satin cloak and the tap, tap, tapping of the cane going off into the distance. But the smell, like every scent in the Garden of Eden, that sweet smell lingered long into the afternoon. . . .

And it has been told that the old man and his sweet wife and their lovely child lived a peaceful and joy-filled life together for many, many years. So may it be for us all. Amen.

The Wise Man and the Apprentice

IRAN/AFGHANISTAN

Once upon a time there was a very wise old man and he lived by himself in a hut made of twigs and grass.

One day a young man came to him and said: "I am an apprentice. Father, if I join you, will you teach me to be wise?"

"My son," said the sage, "I cannot teach you anything. Everything that is any use to one in this world has to be learned by experience."

Nevertheless, the youth vowed to serve the ancient for the rest of his days and begged so hard, saying that he had no father or mother, that the old man allowed him to stay. Day by day, the apprentice, whose name was Abdul, cooked his master's food and tried to learn from his learned discourses.

One day the old man said, "Abdul, I am going on a journey, so I will bid you farewell. Thank you for all you have done for me, but I shall no longer need your services."

Abdul, whose tears now rolled down his face, cried:

"Father, take me with you, for I have vowed to be with you and serve you for the rest of your days."

So the old man relented, and they walked on through the land, receiving food from villagers, and living on that frugal diet quite happily.

But at one village to which they came, the people were not friendly, and threw stones at the old man and boy, saying:

"Leave us in peace, we want no beggars here. Go on your way."

The village dogs followed them yelping and snarling, and even the children mocked them with harsh cries.

The apprentice was very distressed, as he had not eaten for a whole day and was looking forward to a meal when they approached the village. But, as they walked away, the old man did not appear to be unduly worried. And when, on the outskirts of the village, they came to a wall which was falling down, the old man took up stones and some sticks and carefully repaired the wall.

They walked on until nightfall, and then they saw a light among the reeds on the river-bank.

"It is the hut of a fisherman," said the apprentice. "Shall I see if there is something which the owner could spare us to eat?"

"Yes," said the wise man. "We could stay here and rest."

When they knocked on the door there was only a poor old woman at home, who told them that her son, the fisherman, had been taken away by order of the King for the army. Their boat, in which she used to ferry people across the river, was her only means of livelihood, but, she said, they were welcome to some of her soup. After they had both had a bowl of warm soup, the old man and the boy lay down outside, against the oven, and fell asleep.

When it was morning, the old woman gave them some goat's milk and a piece of bread with her blessing. She then ferried them across the river, and after the wise man had given her a few pence, she returned to the other side. As soon as she had tied up the boat and gone inside the hut, the wise man picked up some heavy stones and began to pelt the boat with them.

"Father! What are you doing?" cried Abdul in horror. "You are sinking the old woman's boat! She will not be able to earn a few pence while her son is in the army, and she will starve!"

"No, no, have no fear," said the sage, "it is all for the best." And he trudged on silently for the next few hours.

But the apprentice was heartbroken at his master's behaviour, and resolved to leave him at the next possible opportunity.

When they reached a caravanserai, where camels and donkeys were being stabled for the night, the old man spoke:

"My son, you are not happy. Tell me what it is," said he.

The apprentice stammered:

"I cannot understand. I am afraid I must leave you, for you have done such strange things. First, you mended the wall of the bad villagers who stoned us and reviled us. Then you broke the boat of the old woman who was so kind to us and shared her soup and goat's milk with us. Why have you done this—what does it mean?"

"There was a reason in both cases," said the old man.

"Please tell me the reason, so that I can leave you happier in mind than I am at the moment," pleaded Abdul.

"In the wall which was broken there happened to be a treasure of golden coins," said the sage slowly, "and if the wall had fallen down the bad villagers would have got the treasure. But they were not yet ready, so I mended the wall."

"But the old woman, what about her?"

"In the case of the old woman, it was thus: The soldiers of the King have been scouring the countryside for boats of all kinds and descriptions. Now, tomorrow it is possible that as the old woman's boat is at the bottom of the river it will escape the search. Later, her son will come back from the army, raise the boat and mend it. But if the soldiers had taken it, there would have been nothing left to her. So now you see the reasons which explain my conduct in these two instances."

The apprentice begged the old man's forgiveness, and told him that he would not query again whatsoever he might do. So the old man forgave him and Abdul stayed with him until the end of his days.

The Poppet Caught a Thief

UNITED STATES

One time the people that was sleeping in a tavern all got robbed. It looked like somebody must have put powders in the liquor, and stole their stuff while they was asleep. There wasn't no banks in them days, so travelers had to carry their money in gold. They claimed there was three thousand dollars missing, besides four good watches and a snuffbox which the man says he wouldn't have took a hundred dollars for it. The fellow that run the tavern would not let nobody leave, neither. "Them valuables must be got back, or else I will wade knee-deep in blood," he says, "because the honor of my house has been throwed in jeopardy!"

The travelers was getting pretty mad, but just then an old woman come along and she says, "What is the matter?" The tavernkeeper he told her, and the old woman says, "My poppet can catch any thief in the world, and it won't take ten minutes." She pulled a little wooden doll out of her saddle-bag, and rubbed some walnut-juice on it, and set it on a stand-table. "Them travelers can come in here one at a time," she says, "and the rest of us will set just outside the door. Every one of 'em must grab that there poppet and squeeze it. If the man's honest you won't hear a sound, but if he's a thief the poppet will holler like a stuck pig." The travelers says it is all foolishness, but they will try anything to get away from this lousy tavern. So they went in one after another, but the poppet didn't holler at all.

The old woman looked considerable set back. "Did you all pinch the poppet?" she asked. The travelers all says they squeezed it hard as they could. "Hold out your hands," says the old woman, and she studied each man's fingers mighty careful. Pretty soon she pointed at the traveler that done all the hollering about his snuffbox. "That's the thief," she says. The fellow tried to lie out of it, but when they got the rope around his neck he begun to holler. "If you turn me loose I will give everything back," says he. "But if you hang me you will never get a penny, because that gold is hid where you couldn't find it in a thousand years." Well, the tavernkeeper was unanimous for hanging him anyhow, but them travelers naturally wanted to get their money back. They promised to put the robber on a good horse and give him three hours' start. He made everybody swear with their right hand on the Book, and then he showed them where the stuff was hid under a woodpile. So pretty soon they turned the son-of-a-gun loose, and off he went down the road at a dead run. Nobody ever did catch up with him, neither.

Soon as the people got their money and watches, they begun to feel pretty good again. The tavernkeeper set up a big dinner, and everybody eat and drunk till they was full as a tick. Pretty soon they raffled off the robber's watch to pay for the dinner, and the man that won the watch give it to the old woman. Finally a fellow passed the old woman's bonnet around for a silver collection, and then he says, "You can have all this money, if you will tell us how you knowed which one was the thief."

The old woman just grinned at him. "Didn't you hear my poppet holler, when that scoundrel grabbed it?" she says. The fellow says of course not, and everybody knows a wooden doll can't holler. "A thief don't know nothing for sure," says the old woman. "Every one of you honest men squeezed that poppet. But the robber figured there might be a trick to it, so he never touched the poppet. All I done was to look for the fellow that didn't have no walnut juice on his hands."

Trickery

In many cultures, the trickster character is a figure of chaos: Coyote, Raven, Loki, Anansi, Br'er Rabbit, Robin Goodfellow, Maui. This is the elemental trickster, the one Alan Garner says "is the advocate of uncertainty . . . at once creator and destroyer, bringer of help and harm." Joseph Campbell calls the great tricksters "super shamans."

The following tales of trickery, however, are closer to wisdom stories and classic scams than the great trickster cycles. Here an old man or an old woman gets the better of a husband or wife or thief or giant or master—or the Devil himself.

The Clever Old Man

In a certain village there lived seven brothers. They all lived by thieving and burgling. They lived separately but always worked as a team. One day the eldest said, "Brothers, that old man there has plenty of money. Let us burgle his place tomorrow." The others agreed.

The old man then had a dream that these men would pay a visit to his house the next day. When he woke up he said to his wife, "Old woman, I'll tell you what! Have we got a fair quantity of rice-beer?" When she said that they had, he said, "Well then, tomorrow at noon you must cook for seven people and keep your dishes of meat and rice ready. Cook *matimah* [pulse] too. When the visitors arrive, ask them to sit down so that you can serve them a meal. I will go out in the morning to the field and take our pet paddy-bird with me. But I will be back by noon."

Next morning the old man was plowing his field. The pet paddy-bird sat close by looking for frogs. Soon the seven thieves came along and, seeing the old man, they accosted him thus: "Grandfather, what are you doing?" The old man answered, "My sons, I have got to feed my old lady, hence I am driving this plow. But which way are you bound?" They said, "We plan to visit your house." "That's very well," replied the old man. He then addressed his pet, saying "Paddy-bird, go home and tell grandmother to kill the fowl and prepare food for seven guests." He then drove his bird off with a stick and it flew back home.

After a time the old man and his guests reached home. The old lady had kept everything ready. The thieves were surprised to find such a good meal, and they thought that she had prepared all these things because she had received the bird's message. After the meal was over they thought that they could also use the services of such a bird. Then they too could have timely and fine meals. When the old man asked them, "My boys, what made you come to my place?" they answered, "Grandfather, we want this bird." The old man then said, "No, I can't give up my bird. It is our mainstay. It's because of it that we two are still alive." But the thieves were keen on the bird and would not leave without it. In fact, they took it away by force.

Soon the time came to try out the bird. So the eldest thief took it to a field. When it was about noon he raised a stick over the head of the paddy-bird and said, "Go, tell my wife to cook a fowl and to keep some rice-beer ready." But when he returned home he found that his wife had not cooked anything. There was only leftover rice from the last night's meal. However, the thief was hungry and ate whatever he was given. Then he took the bird to his next younger brother. The latter then asked him, "How did you find our new bird?" "Oh, it was all right," he replied. "I gave it a message and my wife prepared rice, meat, and rice-beer for me. I had a hearty meal." The younger brother then sent the bird from his field with the message: "Go, and tell my wife to prepare some rice, meat, and rice-beer." However, instead of a warm and rich meal he too had only leftover rice to eat. This man then passed the bird on to his younger brother. In this way each of the brothers tried the bird and each found himself cheated. The youngest brother, in fact, soon blurted out, "Why, we have been had by this old fellow." The others agreed.

One evening they planned something new: "We will go tomorrow and tie up the old man and take all his money and gold." That night the old man had another dream. Again he came to know of their plans. He said to his wife, "Old woman, those men are coming again. Please keep a meal ready as before. Prepare some rice-beer, too. Strip a piece of banana tree bark and put it in the room where we pray to the goddess of wealth. And please place a stick of mature bamboo by my seat. Then go and borrow our neighbor's daughter saying that she is needed to help you. Keep her hidden in the room belonging to the Goddess Mainao [the goddess of wealth]. But you have to do more. While serving our guests rice you must pretend to slip on the floor because you accidentally trod on one of their leaf-plates. Leave the rest to me."

After giving all these instructions, the man went out with his plow early in the morning. After a time the thieves came along and the old man now addressed them saying, "My sons, which way are you going?" They answered, "We are going to your house, grandfather." The old man then replied, "Very well. But please wait while I finish my plowing." So after a while they followed the old man to his house. The old woman then brought out the rice-beer. After all of them had sat down to eat, the old lady pretended to let her foot slip on the leaf-plate of one of the guests. The old man then immediately took the stick and waving it at his wife he began to roar, "You old woman, don't you see with your eyes! Though you are old you don't know how to behave! Let me turn you into a young girl!" So saying, he began to strike the piece of bark from the banana tree. After a while a young girl came to serve rice and curry. The thieves were impressed beyond measure with the magic virtues of the old man's stick. How wonderful! It could change even an old lady into a comely girl! They then forgot the mission with which they had come and asked the old man for his stick. But he would not agree to part with it, so they took it by force.

Then the eldest thief thought, "My wife is already old, let me turn her into a young woman." He thus began to beat her, saying, "Be young, be young." The heavy stick was too much for the woman, however, and she lost her life. The thief then hid her body and passed the stick to his next younger brother, saying, "My wife has turned into a young woman." The second brother's wife also lost her life in the same way. Indeed, soon all their wives had died, but when the youngest one's wife lost her life, he began to cry aloud. The other brothers then admitted sorrowfully that their wives, too, were dead. They now worried constantly about how to manage their children and run their homes. They hadn't the means to marry again and now became more determined than ever to rob the old man of his wealth. They decided they would not be dissuaded again from their purpose.

Again the old man had a dream and came to know of their plan. So he instructed his wife, saying, "Old woman, do you see that nest of hornets in the banana tree? Detach it from the tree carefully and keep it in a corner on the veranda. When I say to you: 'Old woman, where have you kept our money? I seem to have forgotten where it is,' you must answer, 'Why, it is there in the pitcher in the corner of the veranda.'" The thieves arrived that very evening. The old man started drinking rice-beer when he saw them, and as if intoxicated, he soon cried out, "Old woman, I seem to have forgotten where the money is kept. Where is it?" She responded, "You old fellow, you have forgotten everything by drinking so much rice-beer. Why, it's there in the pitcher in the corner." The thieves overheard this and were happy that they were at last going to have the old man's money. So the eldest thief went up to the hornet's nest. As he put in his hand the hornets stung him on his hands and face. He stepped back quickly and the next brother then went up and put his hand in, with the same result. None cried out, each appearing as if he had pulled out money from the pitcher. In this way, one after another, all the men were severely stung by these ferocious hornets. As they left, however, the youngest brother cried out, "Ah, how severely was I stung! Oh, brothers, I am half dead with pain!" The older brothers then admitted how much they had suffered too.

After a few days, when their pain had subsided, the thieves again planned to pay a visit to the old man's house. But he came to know of their plans as before. So he now said to his wife, "Old woman, make a small hole in the wall. I will lie by that hole with a razor in my hand. Prepare a paste of some rotten fish and rub me with it so that I stink. Keep some hot chili paste by the granary as well. When they arrive, start wailing. Say that I am dead, and when they question you, ask them to smell me through the hole to see if I am dead or not."

When the thieves arrived the old woman began to wail. When they asked her why she was wailing she said, "Ah, my sons, the old man is no more. These seven days he has been rotting in the house because there's no one to carry him away. I am passing my mornings and evenings by wailing." They then asked, "Where's the body lying?" She answered, "Why, in there! You can smell him through that hole." So the eldest thief tried to peep inside. His nose was then quickly cut off. So he stepped away, covered his nose, and said, "Ah, what a disgusting stench!" Then the next brother peeped in. His nose was cut off too. He also stepped back, saying, "What a disgusting stench!" In this way, one after another, all the men lost their noses. But when it came to the youngest he cried out, "Alas, my nose is no more!" The other brothers then admitted that their noses were gone also. In the meantime the old man cried but from inside the house, "Old woman, that fine salve I've put there don't give it to those rogues; don't let them have it!" The men then went directly up to the chili paste and rubbed it on their wounds. They could now hardly stand the burning and smarting this paste gave them. Roaring in pain, they left for home and promised that they would no longer depend on thieving and burgling for a living but would try to lead an honest life.

How Grandpa Mowed
the Lord's Meadow

A rich lord hired grandpa to mow his hay for twenty-five rubles, and drove him in his horse cart to the distant meadow. There he left him with food enough to last him while he worked.

After the lord had gone, grandpa cooked himself some lunch, ate it, and lay down for a nap. In the evening, as the sun was setting, he woke, had his supper, and went to sleep again. In the morning, as the sun was rising, he woke, cooked his breakfast, ate it, and lay down again.

This went on for seven days. When he had no more food left, grandpa returned to the lord and demanded his wages. But the lord was stingy. He did not want to part with twenty-five rubles and gave grandpa only twenty. Grandpa tried to argue with him, but soon he realized he could not win. Then, with a threatening look, he asked the lord:

"So you won't pay me the rest of my wages?"

"I won't," said the lord.

"Is that final?"

"It is final."

"In that case, let all the grass rise back in its place in the meadow," said grandpa, spat, and walked away.

The lord was happy that he had saved five rubles. He harnessed his horse and drove off to look at his hay. But when he came to the meadow, he found all the grass in its place, even taller and greener than before.

"Oh, what a fool I was!" he cried. "I should have given old grandpa his five rubles. Now I will have to pay again to have it mowed a second time!"

And sly old grandpa went home, grinning, with twenty rubles in his pocket.

Kitta Gray

SWEDEN

Kitta Gray was an ugly but very shrewd old crone. She outsmarted even the Devil himself.

One time she made a bet with him that she could beat him in a footrace. They chose to run through a swamp—it was the swamp down by Klöse in Västergötland, by the way—and Kitta Gray promised that if the Devil won she'd give herself to him.

When the race started, they both ran off into the swamp. Before long Kitta Gray started falling behind, but the Devil didn't notice; he was too busy racing ahead. When he reached the finish line, he was surprised to find the old woman already there, peeking out from behind a bush. Then they ran back again, and the old woman fell behind once more, and the Devil pulled ahead. But when they arrived at the finish line, there she was again, thumbing her nose at him. And they continued on in this way, back and forth, back and forth, until the Devil, who was completely exhausted, finally had to give up.

The fact is that Kitta Gray had a sister who looked so much like her that you couldn't tell them apart, and she and her sister had positioned themselves at either end of the swamp. That was the way Kitta Gray fooled the Devil.

In that same region lived a merchant whose business was doing very poorly. One day the Devil showed up and offered to help him. When the merchant complained that he had no customers no matter how good his merchandise was, the Devil told him that he'd get him so many customers that he wouldn't be able to meet the demand. The merchant didn't believe it; he said that if the day ever came when he ran out of goods to sell, that day the Devil could come for him.

From then on, business began to pick up. One day the merchant saw that he'd sold almost everything. Now he started to get worried, for he realized that he'd sold his soul to the Devil. Then he thought of Kitta Gray. He sent for her and told her how things were. She said, "Make a glass cabinet and put me inside. Then tell people that I'm for sale."

When the Devil arrived, thinking that he was about to claim his victim, he asked the merchant how business was going.

"Very well, except for one item that seems to be terribly hard to sell."

When the Devil asked what it was, the merchant showed

him the cabinet in which Kitta Gray sat laughing. When the Devil saw her, he said, "Anyone who knows Kitta Gray would never, ever buy her."

And he rushed out the door, never to return.

The Devil and the Gipsy

RUSSIA

An old gipsy went to engage himself as servant to a devil; the devil said: "I will give you what you wish to bring me firewood and water regularly, and to put fire under the kettle." "Good!" The devil gave him a pail and said: "Go yonder to the well and draw some water."

Our gipsy went off, got some water into the pail, and drew it up with a hook; but, being old, he couldn't draw it out, and was obliged to pour the water out, in order not to lose the pail in the well. But what was he now to return home with? Well, our gipsy took some stakes out of a fence, and grubbed round about the well, as if he were digging. The devil waited and waited, and as the gipsy didn't appear himself, of course he didn't appear with the water. After awhile he went himself to meet the gipsy, and without thinking inquired: "But why do you loiter so? Why haven't you brought water by this time?" "Well, what? I want to dig out the whole well, and bring it to you!" "But you would have wasted time, if you had purposed anything of the sort; then you wouldn't have brought the pail in time, that the quantity of firewood might not be diminished." And he drew out the water and carried it himself. "Eh! if I had but known, I should have brought it long ago."

The devil sent him once to the wood for firewood. The gipsy started off, but rain assailed him in the wood and wetted him through; the old fellow caught cold and couldn't stoop after the sticks. What was he to do? Well, he took and pulled bast; he pulled several heaps, went round the wood, and tied one tree to another with strips of the bast. The devil waited, waited on, and was out of his wits on account of the gipsy. He went himself, and when he saw what was going on: "What are you doing, loiterer?" said he. "What am I doing? I want to bring you wood. I'm tying the whole forest into one bundle, in order not to do useless work." The devil saw that he was having a bad time of it with the gipsy, took up the firewood, and went home.

After settling his affairs at home, he went to an older devil to ask his advice: "I've hired a gipsy, but he's quite a nuisance; *we're* tolerably cute," says he, "but he's still stronger and cuter than we. Unless I kill him—" "Good, when he lies down to sleep, kill him, that he mayn't lead us by the nose any more." The time came to go home; they lay down to sleep; but the gipsy evidently noticed something, for he placed his fur-coat on the bench where he usually slept, and crept himself into a corner under the bench. When the time came, the devil thought that the gipsy was now in a dead sleep, took up an iron club, and beat the fur-coat till the sound went on all sides. He then lay down to sleep, thinking: "Oho! it's now amen for the gipsy!" But the gipsy grunted: "Oh!" and made a rustling in the corner. "What ails you?" "Oh, a flea bit me." The devil went again to the older one for advice: "But where to kill him?" said he. "When I smashed him with a club, he only made a rustling and said: 'A flea bit me.'" "Then pay him up now," said the elder devil, "as much as he wants, and pack him off about his business." The gipsy chose a bag with ducats and went off. Then the devil was sorry about the money, and consulted the other one again. "Overtake the gipsy, and say that the one of you that kicks a stone best, so that the sound goes three miles, shall have the money." The devil overtook him: "Stay, gipsy! I've something to say to you." "What are you after, son of the enemy?" "Oh, stay, let us kick; the one that kicks loudest against a stone, let his be the money." "Now then, kick away," said the gipsy. The devil kicked once, twice, till it resounded in their ears; but the gipsy meanwhile poured some water on it: "Eh! what's that, you fool?" "When I kick a dry stone, water spurts out." "Ah! when he kicks, tremble! water has spurted out of the stone."

The devil went again for advice. The elder one said: "Let the one who throws the club highest have the money." The gipsy had now got some miles on his way; he looked round; the devil was behind him: "Stop! wait, gipsy!" "What do you want, son of the enemy?" "The one of us that throws the club highest let his be the money." "Well, let us throw now. I've two brothers up yonder in heaven, both smiths, and it will just suit them either for a hammer or for tongs." The devil threw, so that it whizzed, and was scarcely visible. The gipsy took it by the end, scarcely held it up, and shouted:

"Hold out your hands there, brothers—hey!" But the devil seized him by the hand: "Ah, stop! don't throw; it would be a pity to lose it."

The elder devil advised him again: "Overtake him once more, and say, 'The one that runs fastest to a certain point, let him have the money.'" The devil overtook him; the gipsy said: "Do you know what? I shan't contend with you any more, for you don't deserve it; but I've a young son, Hare, who's only just three days old; if you overtake him, you shall measure yourself with me." The gipsy had espied a hare in a firwood: "There he is! little Hare! now, then, Hare! Catch him up!" When the hare started he went hither and thither in bounds, only a line of dust rose behind him. "Bah!" said the devil, "he doesn't run straight." "In my family no one ever did run straight. He runs as he pleases."

The elder devil advised him to wrestle; the stronger was to have the money. "Eh!" said the gipsy; "you hear the terms for me to wrestle with you: I have a father; he is so old that for the last seven years I have carried him food into a cave; if you floor him, then you shall wrestle with me." But the gipsy knew of a bear, and led the devil to his cave. "Go," said he, "in there; wake him up, and wrestle with him." The devil went in and said: "Get up, long-beard! let us have a wrestle." Alas! when the bear began to hug him, when he began to claw him, he beat him out, he turned him out, and threw him down on the floor of the cave.

The elder devil advised that the one who whistled best, so that it could be heard for three miles, should have the money. The devil whistled so that it resounded and whizzed again. But the gipsy said: "Do you know what? When I whistle you will go blind and deaf; bind up your eyes and ears." He did so. The gipsy took a mallet for splitting logs, and banged it once and twice against his ears. "Oh, stop! Oh! don't whistle, or you'll kill me! May ill luck smite you with your money! Go where you will never be heard of again!" That's all.

The Old Woman and the Giant

PHILIPPINES

In a cave near the village of Umang, there once lived a wicked and greedy giant. He would kill and eat anyone who happened to pass by the cave. That was why everybody tried to avoid the place.

But one day, an old woman, who had gone to the woods to gather fuel, lost her way and found herself near the giant's cave. Seeing her, the giant shouted, "Now, I'm going to kill and eat you, unless you can show me that you can make a louder noise than I."

This frightened the old woman. But being wise and shrewd, she kept her head.

"What good will it do you if you eat a skinny old woman like me?" she asked the giant. "But if you let me go, I'll fetch my daughter, who's young and stout. Then, if you can make more noise than the two of us together, you may kill both of us. And you'll really have something good to eat."

The giant's greed was aroused. And so he told the old

woman, "All right, you may go. But be sure to come back and bring your stout daughter with you."

The old woman went home and returned as she had promised, bringing her daughter with her. She had a drum with her, while her daughter had a bronze gong.

As soon as they neared the cave, the old woman began to beat her drum. At the same time, the daughter beat her gong. The noise that they made was so great that the giant could not hear his own voice, no matter how hard he shouted.

When he could no longer stand the noise, the giant covered his ears with his hands. Then he dashed blindly out of the cave. And he fell into a great big hole.

That was the end of the wicked and greedy giant. And the people of the whole countryside rejoiced at his death.

John Fraser the Cook

SCOTLAND

There was a waggish old man cook at Duntrune for sixty years, and during three generations of its owners. In 1745–6, when his master was skulking, John found it necessary to take another service, and hired himself to Mr Wedderburn of Pearsie; but he wearied to get back to Duntrune. One day the Laird of Pearsie observed him putting a spit through a peat—it may have been for the purpose of cleaning it—be that as it may, the laird inquired the reason for so doing, and

John replied, "Indeed, sir, I am just gaein to roast a peat, for fear I forget my trade." At the end of two years he returned to Duntrune, where he continued to exercise his calling till near the close of life.

One day he sent up a roast goose for dinner which he or someone had despoiled of a leg before it came to table; on which his master summoned him from the kitchen to inquire who had taken the leg off the goose. John replied that all the geese here had but ae leg. In corroboration of his assertion, he pointed to a whole flock before the window, who were, happily, sitting asleep on one leg, with a sentinel on the watch. The laird clapped his hands and cried *whew*, on which they got upon both legs, and flew off. But John, no way discomfited, told his master, if he had cried *whew* to the one on the table, it would most likely have done the same!

The Seven Leavenings

PALESTINIAN ARAB

There was once in times past an old woman who lived in a hut all by herself. She had no one at all. One day when the weather was beautiful she said, "Ah, yes! By Allah, today it's sunny and beautiful, and I'm going to take the air by the seashore. But let me first knead this dough."

When she had finished kneading the dough, having added the yeast, she put on her best clothes, saying, "By Allah, I just have to go and take the air by the seashore." Arriving at the seashore, she sat down to rest, and lo! there was a boat, and it was already filling with people.

"Hey, uncle!" she said to the man, the owner of the boat. "Where in Allah's safekeeping might you be going?"

"By Allah, we're heading for Beirut."

"All right, brother. Take me with you."

"Leave me alone, old woman," he said. "The boat's already full, and there's no place for you."

"Fine," she said. "Go. But if you don't take me with you, may your boat get stuck and sink!"

No one paid her any attention, and they set off. But their boat had not gone twenty metres when it started to sink. "Eh!" they exclaimed. "It looks as if that old woman's curse has been heard." Turning back, they called the old woman over and took her with them.

In Beirut, she did not know anybody or anything. It was just before sunset. The passengers went ashore, and she too came down and sat a while, leaning against a wall. What else could she have done? People were passing by, coming and going, and it was getting very late. In a while a man passed by. Everyone was already at home, and here was this woman sitting against the wall.

"What are you doing here, sister?" he asked.

"By Allah, brother," she answered. "I'm not doing anything. I'm a stranger in town, with no one to turn to. I kneaded my dough and leavened it, and came out for pleasure until it rises, when I'll have to go back."

"Fine," he said. "Come home with me then."

He took her home with him. There was no one there except him and his wife. They brought food, laughed and played—you should have seen them enjoying themselves. After they had finished, lo! the man brought a bundle of sticks this big and set to it—Where's the side that hurts most?—until he had broken them on his wife's sides.

"Why are you doing this, grandson?" the old woman asked, approaching in order to block his way.

"Get back!" he said. "You don't know what her sin is. Better stay out of the way!" He kept beating his wife until he had broken the whole bundle.

"You poor woman!" exclaimed the old lady when the man had stopped. "What's your sin, you sad one?"

"By Allah," replied the wife, "I've done nothing, and it hadn't even occurred to me. He says it's because I can't get pregnant and have children."

"Is that all?" asked the old woman. "This one's easy. Listen, and let me tell you. Tomorrow, when he comes to beat you, tell him you're pregnant."

The next day, as usual, the husband came home, bringing with him the needed household goods and a bundle of sticks. After dinner, he came to beat his wife, but he had not hit her with the first stick when she cried out, "Hold your hand! I'm pregnant!"

"Is it true?"

"Yes, by Allah!"

From that day on, he stopped beating her. She was pampered, her husband not letting her get up to do any of the housework. Whatever she desired was brought to her side.

Every day after that the wife came to the old woman and said, "What am I going to do, grandmother? What if he should find out?"

"No matter," the old woman would answer. "Sleep easy. The burning coals of evening turn to ashes in the morning." Daily the old woman stuffed the wife's belly with rags to make it look bigger and said, "Just keep on telling him you're pregnant, and leave it to me. The evening's embers are the morning's ashes."

Now, this man happened to be the sultan, and people heard what was said: "The sultan's wife is pregnant! The sultan's wife is pregnant!" When her time to deliver had come, the wife went to the baker and said, "I want you to bake me a doll in the shape of a baby boy."

"All right," he agreed, and baked her a doll which she wrapped and brought home without her husband seeing her. Then people said, "The sultan's wife is in labour, she's ready to deliver."

The old woman came forth. "Back in my country, I'm a midwife," she said. "She got pregnant as a result of my efforts, and I should be the one to deliver her. I don't want anyone but me to be around."

"Fine," people agreed. In a while, word went out: "She gave birth! She gave birth!"

"And what did she give birth to?"

"She gave birth to a boy."

Wrapping the doll up, the wife placed it in the crib. People were saying, "She gave birth to a boy!" They went up to the sultan and said she had given birth to a boy. The crier made his rounds, announcing to the townspeople that it was forbidden to eat or drink except at the sultan's house for the next week.

Now, the old woman made it known that no one was permitted to see the baby until seven days had passed. On the seventh day it was announced that the sultan's wife and the baby were going to the public baths. Meanwhile, every day the wife asked the old woman, "What am I going to do, grandmother? What if my husband should find out?" And the old woman would reply, "Rest easy, my dear! The evening's coals are the morning's ashes."

On the seventh day the baths were reserved for the sultan's wife. Taking fresh clothes with them, the women went, accompanied by a servant. The sultan's wife went into the bath, and the women set the servant in front of the doll, saying to her, "Take care of the boy! Watch out that some dog doesn't stray in and snatch him away!"

In a while the servant's attention wandered, and a dog came, grabbed the doll, and ran away with it. After him ran the servant, shouting, "Shame on you! Leave the son of my master alone!" But the dog just kept running, munching on the doll.

It is said that there was a man in that city who was suffering from extreme depression. He had been that way for seven years, and no one could cure him. Now, the moment he saw a dog running with a servant fast behind him shouting, "Leave the son of my master alone!" he started to laugh. And he laughed and laughed till his heartsickness melted away and he was well again. Rushing out, he asked her, "What's your story? I see you running behind a dog who has snatched away a doll, and you're shouting at him to leave the son of your master alone. What's going on?"

"Such and such is the story," she answered.

This man had a sister who had just given birth to twin boys seven days before. Sending for her, he said, "Sister, won't you put one of your boys at my disposal?"

"Yes," she said, giving him one of her babies.

The sultan's wife took him and went home. People came to congratulate her. How happy she was!

After some time the old woman said, "You know, grand-children, I think my dough must have risen, and I want to go home and bake the bread."

"Why don't you stay?" they begged her. "You brought blessings with you." I don't know what else they said, but she answered, "No. The land is longing for its people. I want to go home."

They put her on a boat, filling it with gifts, and said, "Go in Allah's safekeeping!"

When she came home, she put her gifts away and rested for a day or two. Then she checked her dough. "Yee, by Al-lah!" she exclaimed. "My dough hasn't risen yet. I'm going to the seashore for a good time." At the shore she sat for a while, and lo! there was a boat.

"Where are you going, uncle?"

"By Allah, we're going to Aleppo," they answered.

"Take me with you."

"Leave me alone, old woman. The boat's full and there's no room."

"If you don't take me with you, may your boat get stuck and sink in the sea!"

They set out, but in a while the boat was about to sink. They returned and called the old lady over, taking her with them. Being a stranger, where was she to go? She sat down by a wall, with people coming and going until late in the evening. After everybody had gone home for the night, a man passed by.

"What are you doing here?"

"By Allah, I'm a stranger in town. I don't know anyone, and here I am, sitting by this wall."

"Is it right you should be sitting here in the street? Come, get up and go home with me."

Getting up, she went with him. Again, there was only he and his wife. They had no children or anybody else. They ate and enjoyed themselves, and everything was fine, but when time came for sleep he fetched a bundle of sticks and beat his wife until he had broken the sticks on her sides. The second day the same thing happened. On the third day the old woman said, "By Allah, I want to find out why this man beats his wife like this."

She asked her, and the wife replied, "By Allah, there's nothing the matter with me, except that once my husband brought home a bunch of black grapes. I put them on a bone-white platter and brought them in. 'Yee!' I said. 'How beautiful is the black on the white!' Then he sprang up and said, 'So! May so-and-so of yours be damned! You've been keeping a black slave for a lover behind my back!' I protested that I had only meant the grapes, but he wouldn't believe me. Every day he brings a bundle of sticks and beats me."

"I'll save you," said the old woman. "Go and buy some black grapes and put them on a bone-white platter."

In the evening, after he had had his dinner, the wife brought the grapes and served them. The old woman then jumped in and said, "Yee! You see, son. By Allah, there's nothing more beautiful than the black on the white!"

"So!" he exclaimed, shaking his head. "It's not only my wife who says this! You're an old lady and say the same thing. It turns out my wife hasn't done anything, and I've been treating her like this!"

"Don't tell me you've been beating her just for that!" exclaimed the old woman. "What! Have you lost your mind? Look here! Don't you see how beautiful are these black grapes on this white plate?"

It is said they became good friends, and the husband stopped beating his wife. Having stayed with them a few more months, the old woman said, "The land has been longing for its people. Maybe my dough has risen by now. I want to go home."

"Stay, old lady!" they said. "You brought us blessings."

"No," she answered. "I want to go home."

They prepared a boat for her and filled it with food and other provisions. She gathered herself together and went home. There, in her own house, after she had sat down, rested, and put her things away, she checked the dough. "By Allah," she said, "it has just begun to rise, and I might as well take it to the baker." She took it to the baker, who baked her bread.

This is my tale, I've told it, and in your hands I leave it.

The Fortune-Teller

RUSSIA

In a certain village there lived an old woman, and she had a son, neither too big nor too small, but not old enough to work in the fields. Things came to such a pass that they had nothing in the larder. So the old woman put on her thinking cap and racked her brains to find a way to make ends meet and have a loaf of bread to eat. She thought and thought, until she had an idea. So she said to the boy: "Go lead away somebody's horses, tether 'em to that there bush and give 'em some hay, then untether 'em again, lead 'em to that there hollow and leave 'em there." Now her son was a smart lad, and no mistake. No sooner did he hear this, than off he went, led away some horses and did what his mother had told him. For it was said of her that she knew more than ordinary folk and could read the cards now and then when asked.

When the owners saw their horses had gone, they went in search of them, hunting high and low, poor devils, but there was not a sign of them. "What are we to do?" they cried. "We must get a fortune-teller to find 'em for us, even though it means paying through the nose." Then they remembered the old woman and said: "Let's go to her and ask her to read the cards; like as not she'll tell us summit about 'em." No sooner said than done. They went to the old woman and said: "Granny, dear. We have heard say that you know more than ordinary folk. That you can read the cards and tell all from 'em like an open book. Then read 'em for us, dear mistress, for our horses are gone." Then the old woman said to them: "My strength is failing, dear masters! I am forever a-wheezing and a-gasping, sirs." But they replied: "Do as we ask, dear mistress! It is not for naught. We shall reward you for your pains."

Shuffling and coughing, she laid out the cards, peered hard at them and although they told her nothing—what of it; hunger is no brother, it teaches you a thing or two—said: "Well, I never! Look here, sirs! It seems your horses are in that there place, tethered to a bush." The owners were over-joyed, rewarded the old woman for her pains and went for look for their beasts. They came to the bush, but there was no sign of the horses, though you could see where they had been tethered 'cause part of a bridle was hanging on the bush and there was lots of hay around. They had been there, but now they were gone. The men were grieved, poor devils, and didn't know what to do. They thought it over and went back to the old woman. If she had found out once, she would tell them again.

So they came to the old woman, who was lying on the stove-bed, a-wheezing and a-gasping like goodness knows what was ailing her. They begged her earnestly to read the cards for them again. She pretended to refuse as before, say-ing: "My strength is failing, I am plagued by old age!"—so that they would give her a bit more for her pains. They promised to begrudge her nothing if the horses were found and give her more than before. So the old woman climbed down from the stove-bed, shuffling and coughing, laid out the cards again, peered hard at them and said: "Go look for them in that there hollow. That's where they are for sure!" The owners rewarded her handsomely for her pains and set off again to look. They reached the hollow and found their horses safe and sound; so they took them and led them home.

After that the stories spread far and wide about the old woman with second sight who could read the cards and tell you surely what would come to pass. These rumours reached a certain rich gentleman who had lost a chest full of money. When he heard about the old fortune-teller, he sent his carriage to bring her to him without delay, no matter how poorly she felt. He also sent his two manservants, Nikolasha and Yemelya (it was they who had pinched their master's money). So they came for the old woman, all but dragged her into the carriage by force and set off home. On the way the old woman began to moan and groan, sighing and muttering to herself: "Oh, dear. If it weren't for no cash and an empty belly I would never be a fortune-teller, riding in a carriage for a fine gentleman to lock me up where the ravens would not take my bones. Alas, alack! No good will come of this!"

Nikolasha overheard her and said: "Hear that, Yemelya! The old girl's talking about us. Looks as if we're for it!" "Steady now, lad," said Yemelya. "Perhaps you just imagined it." But Nikolasha told him: "Listen for yourself, there she goes again." The old woman was scared out of her wits. She sat quiet for a while, then began moaning again: "Oh, dear! If it weren't for no cash and an empty belly this would never have happened!" The lads strained their ears to catch what she was saying. After a bit she went on again about "no cash and an empty belly," blathering all sorts of nonsense. When the lads heard this, they got a real fright. What were they to do? They agreed to ask the old woman not to give them away to their master, because she kept saying: "If it weren't for Nikolasha and Yemelya, this would never have happened." In their excitement the two rascals thought the old woman was talking about Nikolasha and Yemelya, not no cash and an empty belly!

No sooner said than done. They begged the old woman: "Have pity on us, Granny dear, and we'll say prayers for you forever more. Why ruin us and tell the master all? Just don't mention us, keep quiet about it; we'll make it worth your while." Now the old woman was no fool. She put two and two together, and her fear vanished in a trice. "Where did you hide it, my children?" she asked. "It was the Devil himself tempted us to commit such a sin," they wailed. "But where is it?" repeated the old woman. "Where else could we hide it but under the bridge by the mill until the good weather comes." So they reached an agreement and then arrived at the rich gentleman's house. When he saw they had brought the old woman, their master was beside himself with joy. He led her into the house and plied her with all manner of food and drink, whatever she fancied, and when she had eaten and drunk her fill, he asked her to read the cards and find out where his money was. But the old woman had her wits about her and kept saying that her strength was failing and she could hardly stand. "Come now, Granny," said the gentleman. "Make yourself at home, sit down, if you like, or lie down if you don't feel well enough to sit, only read the cards and find out what I asked. And if you can tell me who took my money and I find it again, I'll not only wine and dine you, but reward you handsomely with anything that you fancy."

And so, a-wheezing and a-gasping as if afflicted by some terrible malady, the old woman took the cards, laid them out and peered hard at them, muttering to herself all the time. "Your lost chest is under the bridge by the mill," she said finally. No sooner had he heard the old woman's words, than the gentleman sent Nikolasha and Yemelya to find the money and bring it to him. He did not know it was they who had taken it. So they found it and brought it to their master; and their master was so overjoyed to see his money, that he did not count it, and gave the old woman a hundred rubles straightaway and a nice little present besides, promising not to forget her service to him in the future as well. Then, having entertained her lavishly, he sent her home in his carriage and gave her something for the road as well. On the way Nikolasha and Yemelya thanked the old woman for not betraying them to their master and gave her some money too.

After that the old woman was more famous than ever and settled down to a life of ease with all the bread she wanted, and other fare in abundance, and plenty of livestock too. And she and her son lived and prospered and drank beer and mead. For I was there and drank mead-wine, it touched my lips, but not my tongue.

The Old Woman and the Physician

AESOP

An old Woman, who had become blind, called in a Physician, and promised him, before witnesses, that if he would restore her eyesight, she would give him a most handsome reward, but that if he did not cure her, and her malady remained, he should receive nothing. The agreement being concluded, the Physician tampered from time to time with the old lady's eyes, and meanwhile, bit by bit, carried off her goods. At length after a time he set about the task in earnest and cured her, and thereupon asked for the stipulated fee. But the old Woman, on recovering her sight, saw none of her goods left in the house. When, therefore, the Physician importuned her in vain for payment, and she continually put him off with excuses, he summoned her at last before the Judges. Being now called upon for her defence, she said, "What this man says is true enough; I promised to give him his fee if my sight were restored, and nothing if my eyes continued bad. Now then he says that I am cured, but I say just the contrary; for when my malady first came on, I could see all sorts of furniture and goods in my house; but now, when he says he has restored my sight, I cannot see one jot of either."

He who plays a trick must be prepared to take a joke.

Two Women Overcome Nez Percé Man

NATIVE AMERICAN/COEUR D'ALENE

Two very old women went camping toward the Nez Percé country. They made a camp and cooked a gruel of roots. Just as it began to boil one of the women suddenly looked toward the doorway. She saw one of the enemy peeping in. "Don't look toward the door," she said to her friend. "We are being observed. Let us get angry at each other."

The other woman said in Nez Percé, "You're ugly!" "It is not true!" They stood up to fight, one of them with the pot of boiling mush under her arm. The enemy was on his hands and knees and had his mouth open. As the women, fighting each other, came close to the door, one threw the hot mush in the man's face. He ran, but afterwards they found him dead not far from the door.

The Silver Swindle

CHINA

The art of swindling is becoming ever more ingenious. There was an old man of Chinling who took some silver ingots to the money changer's shop at the North Gate Bridge, intending to exchange them for copper coins. He made a point of haggling over the silver content, talking on and on, until a young man came in from outside. The young man's manner was most respectful. He hailed the old man and said, "Your son had some business in Changchou that I was involved in. He gave me a letter and some silver ingots to deliver to you. I was on my way to your residence when I happened to see you in here." The young man handed over the silver, saluted the old man, and left.

The old man tore open the letter and said to the money changer, "My eyesight is not good enough to read this letter from my son. Could I trouble you to read it to me?" The money changer complied. The letter dealt with petty family matters and closed with the words, "The accompanying ten taels of fine silver is for your household needs." Looking pleased, the old man said, "Why don't you give me back my silver? Never mind about testing the silver content. According to my son's letter, these fine silver ingots he has sent me weigh exactly ten taels, so let's exchange them for the copper cash."

The shopkeeper put the new silver on the scales and saw that its weight was 11.3 taels. He supposed that the son had been too busy to check the weight when he sent the letter and had written ten taels as an approximation. "The old man can't weigh it himself," the shopkeeper reasoned. "I may as well let the error stand and keep the difference." So he gave the old man nine thousand copper cash, the current rate of exchange for ten taels of fine silver.

The old man hauled his coppers away. Soon another customer in the shop began snickering. "It looks like the boss has been cheated. That old man has been a con artist in fake silver for years. I spotted him when he came in, but I was afraid to mention it with him in the shop."

The money changer cut open the silver and found that it was lead inside, which upset him terribly. He thanked the stranger and asked him the old man's address. "He lives about a mile from here," said the customer, "and there's still time to catch up with him. But he's my neighbor, and if he finds out I've given him away, he'll get even somehow. So I'll tell you where to look, but leave me out of it."

Naturally the shopkeeper wanted the man to go with him. "If you'd only take me to the neighborhood and point out his place, you could leave. The old man would never know who told me." The stranger was still reluctant to become involved, but when the shopkeeper offered him three taels of silver, he agreed as if he had no choice.

Together the money changer and the stranger went out of the Han Hsi Gate. Far ahead they could see the old man placing coppers on the counter of a wineshop and drinking with some others. Pointing, the stranger said, "There he is! Grab him quickly; I'm going." The money changer ran into the wineshop, caught hold of the old man, and began to beat him. "You dirty crook! You changed ten taels of silver-coated lead for nine thousand good copper cash."

Everyone gathered around. Unruffled, the old man said, "I exchanged ten taels of silver that my son sent me. There was no lead hidden inside. Since you claim that I used fake silver, show it to me."

The money changer held up the split ingot. The old man smiled. "This isn't mine," he said. "I had only ten taels, so I got nine thousand coppers in exchange. This fake silver seems to weigh more than ten taels; it's not the silver I had to begin with. The money changer has come to swindle *me!*"

The people in the wineshop fetched scales to weigh the silver, which indeed came to 11.3 taels. Turning angry, the crowd ganged up on the money changer and beat him. Thus for a moment's greed he fell into the old man's trap. He went home bruised and burning with resentment.

The Straw Ox

RUSSIAN COSSACK

There was once upon a time an old man and an old woman. The old man worked in the fields as a pitch-burner, while the old woman sat at home and spun flax. They were so poor that they could save nothing at all; all their earnings went in bare food, and when that was gone there was nothing left. At last the old woman had a good idea. "Look now, husband," cried she, "make me a straw ox, and smear it all over with tar."

"Why, you foolish woman!" said he, "what's the good of an ox of that sort?"

"Never mind," said she, "you just make it. I know what I am about." What was the poor man to do? He set to work and made the ox of straw, and smeared it all over with tar.

The night passed away, and at early dawn the old woman took her distaff, and drove the straw ox out into the steppe to graze, and she herself sat down behind a hillock, and began spinning her flax, and cried,

"Graze away, little ox, while I spin my flax!
Graze away, little ox, while I spin my flax!"

And while she spun, her head drooped down, and she began to doze, and while she was dozing, from behind the dark wood and from the back of the huge pines a bear came rushing out upon the ox and said, "Who are you? Speak and tell me!"

And the ox said, "A three-year-old heifer am I, made of straw and smeared with tar."

"Oh!" said the bear, "stuffed with straw and smeared with tar, are you? Then give me of your straw and tar, that I may patch up my ragged fur again!"

"Take some," said the ox, and the bear fell upon him and began to tear away at the tar. He tore and tore, and buried his teeth in it till he found he couldn't let go again. He tugged and he tugged, but it was no good, and the ox dragged him gradually off goodness knows where. Then the old woman awoke and there was no ox to be seen. "Alas! old fool that I am!" cried she, "perchance it has gone home." Then she quickly caught up her distaff and spinning board, threw them over her shoulders, and hastened off home, and she saw that the ox had dragged the bear up to the fence, and in she went to the old man. "Dad, dad!" she cried, "look, look! the ox has brought us a bear. Come out and kill it!" Then the old man jumped up, tore off the bear, tied him up, and threw him in the cellar.

Next morning, between dark and dawn, the old woman took her distaff and drove the ox into the steppe to graze. She herself sat down by a mound, began spinning, and said,

"Graze, graze away, little ox, while I spin my flax!
Graze, graze away, little ox, while I spin my flax!"

And while she spun, her head drooped down and she dozed. And, lo! from behind the dark wood, from the back of the huge pines, a grey wolf came rushing out upon the ox and said, "Who are you? Come, tell me!"

"I am a three-year-old heifer, stuffed with straw and trimmed with tar," said the ox.

"Oh! trimmed with tar, are you? Then give me of your tar to tar my sides, that the dogs and the sons of dogs tear me not!"

"Take some," said the ox. And with that the wolf fell upon him and tried to tear the tar off. He tugged and tugged, and tore with his teeth, but could get none off. Then he tried to let go, and couldn't; tug and worry as he might, it was no good. When the old woman woke, there was no heifer in sight. "Maybe my heifer has gone home!" she cried; "I'll go home and see." When she got there she was astonished, for by the palings stood the ox with the wolf still tugging at it. She ran and told her old man, and her old man came and threw the wolf into the cellar also.

On the third day the old woman again drove her ox into the pastures to graze, and sat down by a mound and dozed off. Then a fox came running up. "Who are you?" it asked the ox.

"I'm a three-year-old heifer, stuffed with straw and daubed with tar."

"Then give me some of your tar to smear my sides with, when those dogs and sons of dogs tear my hide!"

"Take some," said the ox. Then the fox fastened her teeth in him and couldn't draw them out again. The old woman told her old man, and he took and cast the fox into the cellar in the same way. And after that they caught Pussy Swift-foot likewise.

So when he had got them all safely, the old man sat down on a bench before the cellar and began sharpening a knife. And the bear said to him:

"Tell me, daddy, what are you sharpening your knife for?"

"To flay your skin off, that I may make a leather jacket for myself and a pelisse for my old wife."

"Oh! don't flay me, daddy dear! Rather let me go, and I'll bring you a lot of honey."

"Very well, see you do it," and he unbound and let the bear go. Then he sat down on the bench and again began sharpening his knife. And the wolf asked him, "Daddy, what are you sharpening your knife for?" "To flay off your skin, that I may make me a warm cap against the winter."

"Oh! don't flay me, daddy dear, and I'll bring you a whole herd of little sheep."

"Well, see that you do it," and he let the wolf go. Then he sat down and began sharpening his knife again. The fox put out her little snout and asked him, "Be so kind, dear daddy, and tell me why you are sharpening your knife!"

"Little foxes," said the old man, "have nice skins that do capitally for collars and trimmings, and I want to skin you!"

"Oh! don't take my skin away, daddy dear, and I will bring you hens and geese."

"Very well, see that you do it!" and he let the fox go. The hare now alone remained, and the old man began sharpening his knife on the hare's account. "Why do you do that?" asked puss, and he replied:

"Little hares have nice little soft warm skins, which will make me gloves and mittens against the winter!"

"Oh, daddy dear! don't flay me, and I'll bring you kale and good cauliflower, if only you let me go!" Then he let the hare go also.

Then they went to bed, but very early in the morning, when it was neither dusk nor dawn, there was a noise in the doorway like "Durrrrrr!"

"Daddy," cried the old woman, "there's some one scratching at the door, go and see who it is!" The old man went out, and there was the bear carrying a whole hive full of honey. The old man took the honey from the bear, but no sooner did he lie down than again there was another "Durrrrrr!" at the door. The old man looked out and saw the wolf driving a whole flock of sheep into the yard. Close on his heels came the fox, driving before him geese and hens and all manner of fowls; and last of all came the hare, bringing cabbage and kale and all manner of good food. And the old man was glad, and the old woman was glad. And the old man sold the sheep and oxen and got so rich that he needed nothing more. As for the straw-stuffed ox, it stood in the sun till it fell to pieces.

The Two Old Women's Bet

One time there were two old women got to talkin' about the men folks: how foolish they could act, and what was the craziest fool thing their husbands had ever done. And they got to arguin', so fin'lly they made a bet which one could make the biggest fool of her husband.

So one of 'em said to her man when he come in from work that evenin', says, "Old man, do you feel all right?"

"Yes," he says, "I feel fine."

"Well," she told him, "you sure do look awful puny."

Next mornin' she woke him up, says, "Stick out your tongue, old man." He stuck his tongue out, and she looked at it hard, says, "Law me! you better stay in the bed today. You must be real sick from the look of your tongue."

Went and reached up on the fireboard, got down all the bottles of medicine and tonic was there and dosed the old man out of every bottle. Made him stay in the bed several days and she kept on talkin' to him about how sick he must be. Dosed him every few minutes and wouldn't feed him nothin' but mush.

Came in one mornin', sat down by the bed, and looked at him real pitiful, started in snifflin' and wipin' her eyes on her apron, says, "Well, honey, I'll sure miss ye when you're gone." Sniffed some more, says, "I done had your coffin made."

And in a few days she had 'em bring the coffin right on in beside the old man's bed. Talked at the old man till she had him thinkin' he was sure 'nough dead. And fin'lly they laid him out, and got everything fixed for the buryin'.

Well, the day that old woman had started a-talkin' her old man into his coffin, the other'n she had gone on to her house and about the time her old man came in from work she had got out her spinnin' wheel and went to whirlin' it. There wasn't a scrap of wool on the spindle, and the old man he fin'lly looked over there and took notice of her, says, "What in the world are ye doin', old woman?"

"Spinnin'," she told him, and 'fore he could say anything she says, "Yes, the finest thread I ever spun. Hit's wool from virgin sheep, and they tell me anybody that's been tellin' his wife any lies can't see the thread."

So the old man he come on over there and looked at the spindle, says, "Yes, indeed, hit surely is mighty fine thread."

Well, the old woman she'd be there at her wheel every time her old man come in from the field—spin and wind, spin and wind, and every now and then take the shuck off the spindle like it was full of thread and lay it in a box. Then one day the old man come in and she was foolin' with her loom, says, "Got it all warped off today. Just got done threadin' it on the loom." And directly she sot down and started in weavin'—step on the treadles, throwin' the shuttle and hit empty. The old man he'd come and look and tell her what fine cloth it was, and the old woman she 'uld weave right on. Made him think she was workin' day and night. Then one evenin' she took hold on the beam and made the old man help her unwind the cloth.

"Lay it on the table, old man—Look out! You're a-lettin' it drag the floor."

Then she took her scissors and went to cuttin'.

"What you makin', old woman?"

"Makin' you the finest suit of clothes you ever had."

Got out a needle directly and sat down like she was sewin'. And there she was, every time the old man got back to the house, workin' that needle back and forth. So he come in one evenin' and she says to him, "Try on the britches, old man. Here." The old man he shucked off his overalls and made like he was puttin' on the new britches.

"Here's your new shirt," she told him, and he pulled off his old one and did his arms this-a-way and that-a-way gettin' into his fine new shirt. "Button it up, old man." And he put his fingers up to his throat and fiddled 'em right on down.

"Now," she says, "let's see does the coat fit ye." And she come at him with her hands up like she was holdin' out his coat for him, so he backed up to her and stuck his arms in his fine new coat.

"Stand off there now, and let me see is it all right.—Yes, it's just fine. You sure do look good."

And the old man stood there with nothin' on but his shoes and his hat and his long underwear.

Well, about that time the other old man's funeral was appointed and everybody in the settlement started for the buryin' ground. The grave was all dug and the preacher was there, and here came the coffin in a wagon, and fin'lly the crowd started gatherin'. And pretty soon that old man with the fine new suit of clothes came in sight. Well, everybody's eyes popped open, and they didn't know whether they ought to laugh or not but the kids went to gigglin' and about the time that old man got fairly close one feller laughed right out, and then they all throwed their heads back and laughed good. And the old man he 'uld try to tell somebody about his fine new suit of clothes, and then the preacher busted out laughin' and slappin' his knee—and everybody got to laughin' and hollerin' so hard the dead man sat up to see what was goin' on. Some of 'em broke and ran when the corpse rose up like that, but they saw him start in laughin'—laughed so hard he nearly fell out the coffin—so they all came back to find out what-'n-all was goin' on.

The two old women had started in quarrelin' about which one had won the bet, and the man in the coffin heard 'em; and when he could stop laughin' long enough he told 'em, says, "Don't lay it on me, ladies! He's got me beat a mile!"

The Fisherman and the Genie

ARABIAN NIGHTS

There once was an aged fisherman, who was so poor that he could scarcely earn as much as would maintain himself, his wife, and three children. He went early every day to fish in the morning, and imposed it as a law upon himself not to cast his nets above four times a day. He went one morning before the moon had set, and, coming to the seaside, undressed himself. Three times did he cast his net, and each time he made a heavy haul. Yet, to his indescribable disappointment and despair, the first proved to be an ass, the second a basket full of stones, and the third a mass of mud and shells.

As daylight now began to appear he said his prayers and commended himself and his needs to his Creator. Having done this, he cast his nets the fourth time, and drew them as formerly, with great difficulty. But, instead of fish, he found nothing in them but a vessel made of yellow copper, having the impression of a seal upon its leaden cover.

This turn of fortune rejoiced him. "I will sell it," said he, "to the smelter, and with the money buy a measure of corn."

He examined the vessel on all sides, and shook it, to see if its contents made any noise, but heard nothing. This circumstance, together with the impression of the seal upon the leaden cover, made him think it enclosed something precious. To satisfy himself, he took his knife and pried open the lid. He turned the mouth downward, but to his surprise, nothing came out. He placed it before him, and while he sat gazing at it attentively, there came forth a very thick smoke, which made him step back two or three paces.

The smoke rose to the clouds, and, spreading itself along the sea and upon the shore, formed a great mist, which we may well imagine filled the fisherman with astonishment. When the smoke was all out of the vessel, it re-formed, and became a solid mass, which changed before his eyes into a genie twice as high as the greatest of giants. At the sight of such a monster, the fisherman would have fled, but was so frightened that he could not move.

The genie regarded the fisherman with a fierce look, and exclaimed in a terrible voice, "Prepare to die, for I will surely kill thee."

"Ah!" replied the fisherman, "why would you kill me? Did I not just now set you at liberty, and have you already forgotten my kindness?"

"Yes, I remember it," said the genie, "but that shall not save thy life. I have only one favor to grant thee."

"And what is that?" asked the fisherman.

"It is," answered the genie, "to give thee thy choice, in what manner thou wouldst have me put thee to death."

"But how have I offended you?" demanded the fisherman. "Is that your reward for the service I have rendered you?"

"I cannot treat thee otherwise," said the genie. "And that thou mayest know the reason, listen to my story.

"I am one of those rebellious spirits that opposed the will of Heaven.

"Solomon, the son of David, commanded me to acknowledge his power, and to submit to his commands. I refused, and told him I would rather expose myself to his resentment than swear fealty as he required. To punish me, he shut me up in this copper vessel. And that I might not break my prison, he himself stamped upon this leaden cover his seal with the great name of God engraved upon it. He then gave the vessel to a genie, with orders to throw me into the sea.

"During the first hundred years of my imprisonment, I swore that if anyone should deliver me before the expiration of that period I would make him rich.

"During the second, I made an oath that I would open all

the treasures of the earth to anyone that might set me at liberty.

"In the third, I promised to make my deliverer a potent monarch, to be always near him in spirit and to grant him every day three requests, of whatsoever nature they might be.

"At last, being angry to find myself a prisoner so long, I swore that if anyone should deliver me I would kill him without mercy, and grant him no other favor than to choose the manner of his death. And therefore, since thou hast delivered me today, I give thee that choice."

The fisherman was extremely grieved, not so much for himself, as on account of his three children; and bewailed the misery to which they must be reduced by his death. He tried to appease the genie, and said, "Alas! take pity on me in consideration of the service I have done you."

"I have told thee already," replied the genie, "it is for that very reason I must kill thee. Do not lose time. All thy reasonings shall not divert me from my purpose. Make haste, and tell me what manner of death thou preferrest?"

Necessity is the mother of invention. The fisherman bethought himself of a stratagem. "Since I must die then," said he to the genie, "I submit to the will of Heaven. But before I choose the manner of my death, I conjure you by the great name which was engraved upon the seal of the prophet Solomon, the son of David, to answer me truly the question I am going to ask you."

The genie, finding himself obliged to make a positive answer by this adjuration, trembled. Then he replied to the fisherman, "Ask what thou wilt, but make haste."

"I wish to know," asked the fisherman, "if you were

actually in this vessel. Dare you swear it by the name of the great God?"

"Yes," replied the genie, "I do swear, by that great name, that I was."

"In good faith," answered the fisherman, "I cannot believe you. The vessel is not capable of holding one of your stature, and how is it possible that your whole body could lie in it?"

"Is it possible," replied the genie, "that thou dost not believe me after the solemn oath I have taken?"

"Truly not I," said the fisherman. "Nor will I believe you, unless you go into the vessel again."

Thereupon the body of the genie dissolved and changed itself into smoke, extending as before upon the seashore. And at last, being collected, it began to re-enter the vessel, which it continued to do till no part remained outside. Immediately the fisherman took the cover of lead, and speedily replaced it on the vessel.

"Genie," cried he, "now it is your turn to beg my favor. But I shall throw you into the sea, whence I took you. Then I will build a house upon the shore, where I will live and tell all fishermen who come to throw in their nets, to beware of such a wicked genie as you are, who has made an oath to kill the person who sets you at liberty."

The Five Wolves

An old woman and her grandson lived near a river. The grandson wished to cross the river, and called the Deer to take him across. Finally an old buck allowed him to mount his back, and carried him across. While they were in the water, the boy cut the throat of the buck with a flint knife and killed him.

The old woman skinned the buck. Five wolves took the scent of the meat, and came intending to steal it. The old woman dressed a piece of rotten wood in skins, and made it look like the boy. Then she wished herself, her grandson, and the meat to be carried to a ledge on the face of a cliff. This cliff is pointed out close to the Okanagon River, near Oroville, Wash. When the wolves arrived, they attacked the tent, but found that what they believed was a boy was only rotten wood. They were unable to reach the ledge. They tried to jump up, but soon wearied. Then they begged for some of the meat. The grandmother told the boy to wrap a hot stone in some suet. He threw it down into the mouth of one of the wolves, and thus killed him. Thus all were killed except the youngest. When he caught the hot stone, he could not swallow it, and the fat burned the sides of his mouth. Therefore wolves have dark marks at the side of the mouth.

The grandmother and the boy continued to live on the ledge. Finally the boy had used up all his arrows, and had no feathers to make new ones. In order to obtain feathers, he caused the golden eagle and the eagle Sinaken to quarrel by telling one that the other one claimed to be swifter and stronger than he. The two eagles fought, and the boy gathered their feathers. He told his grandmother that he would join the people who were going to make war on the sky. He was transformed into a chickadee.

The Crafty Woman

LITHUANIA

A man and his young wife, who had settled down to life in a village, agreed so well that neither of them pronounced a single unpleasant word, they only caressed and kissed each other. For fully six months the Devil did his best to make the pair quarrel, but, at last, irritated by continued failure, he expressed his rage by making a disagreeable noise in his throat and made ready to depart. However, an old woman who was roaming about met him and said, "Why are you annoyed?" The Devil explained, and the woman, on the understanding that she would receive some new bast shoes and a pair of boots, endeavoured to make the young couple disagree. She went to the wife while the husband was at work in the fields and, having begged for alms, said, "Ah, my dear! how pretty and good you are! Your husband ought to love you from the depths of his soul. I know you live more amicably than any other couple in the world, but, my daughter! I will teach you to be yet happier. Upon your husband's head, at the very summit, are a few grey hairs, you must cut them off, taking care that he does not notice what you are about."

"But how shall I do that?"

"When you have given your husband his dinner, tell him to lie down and rest his head upon your lap, then as soon as he goes to sleep, whip a razor out of your pocket and remove the grey hairs." The young wife thanked her adviser and gave her a present.

The old woman went immediately to the field and warned the husband that a misfortune threatened him, since his amiable wife not only had betrayed him, but intended that afternoon to kill him and later to marry someone richer than himself. When at midday, the wife arrived and, after his meal, placed her husband's head upon her knees, he pretended to be asleep and she took a razor from her pocket in order to remove the grey hairs. Instantly the exasperated man jumped on to his feet and, seizing his wife by the hair, began to abuse and strike her. The Devil saw all and could not believe his eyes; soon he took a long pole, attached loosely to one end of it the promised bast shoes and boots, and without coming close, passed them to the old woman. "I will not on any account approach nearer to you," he said, "lest you should in some way impose upon me, for you really are more crafty and cunning than I am!" Having delivered the boots and bast shoes, the Devil vanished as quickly as if he had been shot from a gun.

The Talking Turkeys

SYRIA

Once when the sultan was sick, he did not leave the palace for thirty days. Finally he recovered and felt well enough to step out. Now, it happened that a sly old woman saw him and hurried into the women's reception hall to congratulate the queen on her husband's regained health.

As she was sitting in the queen's presence, the old woman noticed that there were about a hundred turkeys in the court-yard outside the window. So she said to the sultan's wife, "O queen of our time, can these birds of yours talk?" Naturally, the queen said, "No." "If you let me have them for sixty nights, I'll teach them to speak in seven tongues," said the old woman. The queen agreed to have the birds trained. "But," said the old woman, "I shall need provisions to feed them. One hundred sacks of flour, one measure of nuts, one mea-sure of sugar, and so much of this and so much of that." The queen agreed. She gave the order, and they brought what the old woman had asked for.

When the sixty days were almost past, the old woman went to the queen looking very distressed. She said, "These birds of yours are saying strange things, and much as I beat them they will not change their song." "What are they say-ing?" asked the queen. "They say: 'Tsk! Tsk! The sultan's daughter has a lover!'" said the old woman. The queen now looked distressed. "Kill them at once," she said. "And whatever you do, don't bring them back to the palace!"

The old woman obeyed the queen. She kept the turkeys in her house, dining on them herself and cooking some of them for her son's wedding feast.

The Old Woman and the Fox

INDIA

There once was an old woman who was so old that she had outlived all her relatives. She lived by herself at the edge of a village with her two beloved dogs, Ranga and Bhanga. The only family the old woman had left was her great-granddaughter, who was all grown-up, married, and lived in another village far away from the old woman.

One day, the old woman decided she would go visit her great-granddaughter. She instructed her dogs, "You stay here: make sure you don't wander away from home while I am gone!" Ranga and Bhanga obeyed faithfully.

The old lady was making her way out of the village, tottering along on a bamboo walking-stick, when she met a fox. Wagging his long whiskers, the fox declared, "Hey, old woman, I'm going to eat you!"

"Wait," the old woman begged. "If you eat me now, all you'll get is a mouthful of skin and bones. I am on my way to visit my great-granddaughter, who will feed me delicious food and make me nicely plump. Why don't you wait until I return from my trip?"

The fox agreed. "Okay. Go fatten up, and then I'll eat you."

The old woman continued on her journey. In a little while, she was spotted by a tiger, who exclaimed, "Hey, old woman, I'm going to eat you!"

"You don't want to eat me now," the old woman admonished. "Wait until I return from my great-granddaughter's house. Then I will be nice and fat."

The tiger nodded. "Okay, I'll catch you on your way home."

The old woman went a few more paces, leaning heavily on her walking-stick. Suddenly, a bear leaped out of the forest, crying, "Hey, old woman. I'm going to eat you!"

As before, the old woman asked, "Why would you want to eat me now? Wait until I come back from my great-granddaughter's village."

The bear agreed. "Okay, I'll wait until you put some meat on your old bones."

Finally, the old woman reached her great-granddaughter's house. There, she became so fat eating yogurt and cream that she was almost bursting. She asked her great-granddaughter, "Dearest, how will I go home now? The bear, tiger and fox are waiting expectantly to eat me. What will I do?"

Her great-granddaughter replied, "Don't fear, Granny, I will put you in this hollowed-out gourd, and no one will be able to tell you are inside. That way, you will be able to go home safely."

With these words, the great-granddaughter put the old

woman in a giant gourd shell, along with a bowlful of puffed rice and tamarind to sustain her on her long journey home. Then, she gave the gourd a mighty push and sent it rolling down the path.

As the gourd rolled along, the old woman sang,

> *Rolling gourd, rolling gourd*
> *Old woman's gone*
> *Puffed rice and tamarind*
> *Keep rolling on.*

A little while down the road, the bear was lying in wait for the old woman. He stopped the giant gourd shell, examining it carefully, but found that it was neither the old woman nor something edible. When he heard the gourd saying that the old woman had already gone, he decided to wait no longer, and sent it rolling down the path.

A bit later, the tiger spotted a large gourd tumbling down the road. He stopped it, looking it over carefully. He was surprised to hear the gourd reciting,

> *Rolling gourd, rolling gourd*
> *Old woman's gone*
> *Puffed rice and tamarind*
> *Keep rolling on.*

"That sly old woman evaded me!" the tiger realized. "Oh well, no point waiting any longer." He too gave the gourd a good push and sent it on its way.

The old woman rolled along in her comfortable gourd, all

the while munching on the snacks her great-granddaughter had given her. She merrily continued singing,

> Rolling gourd, rolling gourd
> Old woman's gone
> Puffed rice and tamarind
> Keep rolling on.

In the meantime, the clever fox had been waiting patiently for the old woman to return. He spied the gourd, and soon heard the song. Waggling his whiskers, he thought, "Impossible! A gourd can't talk! I have to see what's inside!" He gave a swift kick and broke open the giant shell. Out tumbled the old woman!

"Hey, old woman!" cried the fox, his eyes glistening in greed. "This time you can't escape! I'm going to eat you!"

"Of course," agreed the old woman, "that's why I'm here! But if I may, I'd like to sing you a song before you eat me."

The fox thought over her offer. "Okay," he finally said, "I don't mind a little music before dinner. I don't sing too badly myself; maybe I can join in."

The old woman gave a satisfied smile, saying, "Let's sit on top of that hillock and make sweet music." And so she sang, "Ranga and Bhanga, come to me. Come, come, quickly!"

Within moments, two enormous dogs were bounding down the path toward the old woman and the fox. The fox took one look at their vicious teeth and ran for his life. Laughing heartily, the roly-poly old woman returned home with her beloved dogs.

Bucca Dhu and Bucca Gwidden

ENGLAND

You must know that there are two buccas. Bucca Dhu is the bad goblin, and Bucca Gwidden is the good one. But Bucca Dhu is much bigger and stronger and fiercer than Bucca Gwidden, who is but a little meek thing, after all.

Now once upon a time there was a gay old woman who lived on a farm with her son and her daughter-in-law. The old woman was very fond of playing cards, and even of dancing and singing, though the son and the daughter-in-law thought she ought to know better at her time of life. Wherever people were gathered together to enjoy themselves, there the old woman would be: if it was card-playing, she would fling down her pennies and play with the rest; if it was dancing, she would tuck up her petticoats and foot it right merrily; and if it was singing, she would bawl away in her cracked voice, till she had everyone laughing.

When these parties were over and she set out to walk back to the farm, she would call at the inn on her way, and take a glass or two of hot toddy to keep out the cold, and that made her sing all the louder. And so she would wander home, through dark night or clear night, or wet night or fine night, with her bonnet over one eye and her shawl trailing, and as merry as a cricket in the hedge.

The son didn't like it, nor yet did the daughter-in-law, for they were very proper sort of people.

"She puts us to shame," they said.

So they decided to give her such a fright that she would never venture out at night again.

One dark night, the daughter-in-law fetched a big sheet and put it over the son's head, and tied it round his neck and wrists. He couldn't see very well inside the sheet, so she took him by the hand and led him to a stile that the old woman had to pass over.

"Stay here by the brush," said the daughter-in-law, "and when your mother clambers up on the top of the stile, jump out and wave your arms and groan. *That'll* scare her! She won't want to go over that stile at night again in a hurry!"

And she went back to the farm, and left him standing under the bush.

He waited a long time. It was a windy night, and the bush creaked and rustled and waved its branches about. The man soon began to wish himself safe home again. It seemed to him that there was something alive behind him in the bush, and he kept turning round, but he couldn't see with the sheet over his head. The more the bush creaked and rustled, the more certain he became that there was something lurking there, and he began to think of all the tales he had heard about the bad Bucca Dhu, with his long claws to scratch with, and his great teeth to bite with, for it was just the kind of night when goblins are abroad.

Every minute that passed, the man was getting more and more fearful, and still there was no sign of the old woman. But at last he heard her coming along the path beyond the stile, hopping from one foot to the other, and singing,

On this black night there's nought to see
But Bucca Dhu and me, and me!

"Now keep thy distance, Bucca Dhu," she called over her shoulder. "I aren't afraid of 'ee!"

And so she scrambled up on the top of the stile.

When her son heard her speaking to Bucca Dhu, his teeth began to chatter, but he leaped out from the bush, and waved his arms inside the sheet, and groaned, just as the daughter-in-law had told him to do.

The old woman sat down on the stile and laughed.

"Well now," says she, "if it ain't good little Bucca Gwidden! But thou'st best run along home, my dear, for that old Bucca Dhu is a-following of me close, and if he catches thee, he'll tear thy eyes out! . . . Here he is, here he is!" she cried, turning to looking back over the stile. "He's getting bigger every minute, and he's in some rage! Run, Bucca Gwidden, run, run for thy life!"

Her son didn't wait to be told twice. He gathered up the sheet about his knees as well as he could, and he ran. And since he couldn't see where he was going, he bumped into trees, and stumbled over stones, and fell down, and scrambled up again, and stumbled again.

The old woman sat on the top of the stile and kicked with her heels and clapped with her hands.

"Run, Bucca Gwidden, run, run, run!" she screamed. "After him, Bucca Dhu, catch him, boy, catch him! Well run, Bucca Gwidden, well run, Bucca Dhu! Tear him, Bucca Dhu! Run, Bucca Gwidden!"

When the briars caught the sheet, the son thought it was

Bucca Dhu's claws were in him, and when he ran against the branches of a tree, he thought it was Bucca Dhu's arms were round him; and all the while he ran, the old woman sat on the top of the stile and screamed for joy. He got home at last, more dead than alive, and the daughter-in-law had just taken the sheet off him, and sat him down before the fire to catch his breath, when the old woman walked in.

"Oh my, oh my, oh my!" says she. "*Such* goings on! I met with Bucca Dhu along the way; and we hadn't gone far together when out from a bush leaps Bucca Gwidden! And that great big bucca he set on the little bucca and chased him for his life! One ran, and t'other ran, and 'twas the merriest chase that ever I did see!

"I can't tell 'ee if Bucca Dhu catched Bucca Gwidden—maybe he did, and maybe he didn't. Nor I can't exactly tell 'ee what Bucca Dhu was dressed in. But sure as I'm alive, Bucca Gwidden was wearing one of our sheets; and believe it or not, son, he had boots on just like thine!"

The son smirked, and the daughter-in-law looked foolish. They saw that the old woman was too clever for them, and they never tried to interfere with her again. So she lived merrily all her days.

Adventure

It is easy to envision the elderly in the role of wise person, and only a bit of a stretch to see them as sly tricksters.

But adventurous heroes? Most of us boggle at the thought, forgetting Jacques Cousteau underwater in years that should have been his dotage, forgetting John Glenn heading out into space in his late seventies, and the woman whose name I have long misplaced who was known as the "climbing granny" going up mountains when she was in her nineties.

Sharon Curtin in her astonishingly lyrical book *Nobody Ever Died of Old Age* writes: "Aging paints every action gray, lies heavy on every movement, imprisons every thought." But she goes on to remind us that "the cellular clock is different for each one of us."

And then I remember: I never went underwater, never went into outer space, never climbed any major mountains at twenty-nine, much less fifty-nine.

Some people are heroes. Some people have adventures. At what age these things occur is irrelevant.

As the following stories show.

Verlioka

RUSSIA

There was once upon a time an old man and an old woman, and they had two orphan grandchildren so lovely, gentle, and good, that the old man and the old woman could not love them enough. The old man once took it into his head to go out into the fields with his grandchildren to look at the peas, and they saw that their peas were growing splendidly. The old man rejoiced at the sight with his grandchildren, and said: "Well, now, you won't find peas like that in the whole world! By and by we'll make kisel out of it, and bake us some pea-cakes." And next morning the grandfather sent the eldest grandchild, and said: "Go and drive away the sparrows from the peas!"

The grandchild sat down beside the peas, shook a dry branch, and kept on saying, "Whish! whish! sparrows, ye have pecked at grandfather's peas till you're quite full!" And all at once she heard a rumbling and a roaring in the wood, and Verlioka came, huge of stature, with one eye, a hooked nose, ragged stubbly hair, moustaches half an ell long, swine's bristles on his head, hobbling on one leg, in a wooden boot, leaning on a crutch, grinding all his teeth, and smiling. He went up to the pretty little grandchild, seized her, and dragged her away with him behind the lake. The grandfather waited and waited, but there was no grandchild; and he sent his young grandson after her. Verlioka walked off with him also. The grandfather waited and waited, and said to his wife: "How very late our grandchildren are! I suppose they are running about there and idling their time away, or catching starlings with some lads or other, and meanwhile, the sparrows are stealing our peas! Go along, old woman, and teach them sense!" The old woman rose from the stove, took her stick from the corner, gave the pasties another turn, went away— and never came back. As soon as Verlioka saw her in the field, he cried: "What dost thou want here, old hag? Hast thou come hither to shell peas? Then I'll make thee stand here among the peas for ever and ever!" Then he set to work be-labouring her with his crutch, till little by little her very soul oozed out of her, and she lay upon the field more dead than alive.

The grandfather waited in vain for his grandchildren and his old wife, and began to scold at them: "Where on earth have they got to?" said he; "'tis a true saying that a man must expect no good from his ribs." Then the old man himself made his way to the peas, and saw the old woman lying on the ground in such a battered condition that he scarcely knew her, and of his grandchildren there was no trace. The grand-father cried aloud, picked up the old woman, dragged her home by degrees, gradually brought her to with a little cold water, and she opened her eyes at last and told the grandfa-ther who it was that had beaten her so, and dragged her grandchildren away from the field. The grandfather was very wroth with Verlioka, and said: "This is too much of a joke! Wait a bit, friend, we also have arms of our own! Look to thyself, Verlioka, and take care that I don't twist thy mous-taches for thee! Thou hast done this thing with thy hand, thou shalt pay for it with thy head!" And as the old grand-mother did not hold him back, the grandfather seized his iron crutch and went off to seek Verlioka.

He went on and on till he came to a little pond, and in the pond was swimming a bob-tailed drake. He saw the grandfather and cried: "Tak, tak, tak! Live for a hundred years, old grandad! I have been waiting here for thee a long time!"—"Hail to thee also, drake! Why has thou been awaiting me?"—"Well, I know that thou art in quest of thy grandchildren, and art going to Verlioka to settle accounts with him!"—"And how dost thou come to know of this monster?"—"Tak, tak, tak!" screeched the drake, "I have good cause to know him; 'twas he who docked my tail!"—"Then canst thou show me his dwelling?"—"Tak, tak, tak!" screeched the drake; "here am I but a little tiny bird, but I'll have my tail's worth out of him, I know!"—"Wilt thou go on before and show me the way? I see thou hast a good noddle of thy own, though thou art bob-tailed!" Then the drake came out of the water and climbed up on the bank, waddling from side to side.

They went on and on, and they came upon a little bit of cord lying in the road, and it said, "Hail, little grandad wise-pate!"—"Hail, little cord!"—"Where dost thou dwell, and whither dost thou wander?"—"I live in such and such a place; I am going to pay off Verlioka; he has beaten my old woman and carried off my two grandchildren, and such splendid grandchildren, too!"—"Take me that I may help!" The grandfather thought: "I may as well take it; it will do to hang Verlioka with." Then he said to the little cord: "Come along with us, if thou dost know the way." And the little cord wriggled after them just as if it were a little tapering snake.

They went on and on, and they saw lying in the road a little water-mill, and it said to them: "Hail, little grandad wise-pate!"—"Hail, little water-mill!"—"Where dost thou dwell, and whither dost thou wander?"—"I live in such and such a place, and I am going to settle accounts with Verlioka. Just fancy! he has beaten my old woman and carried off my grandchildren, and such splendid grandchildren, too!"—"Take me with thee that I may help!" And the grandfather thought: "The water-mill may be of use, too." Then the water-mill raised itself up, pressed against the ground with its handle, and went along after the grandfather.

Again they went on and on, and in the road lay an acorn, and it said to them in a little squeaky voice: "Hail, grandad long-nose!"—"Hail, oakey acorn!"—"Whither art thou striding away like that?"—"I am going to beat Verlioka; dost know him?"—"I should think I did; take me with thee to help!"—"But how canst thou help?" Then the grandfather thought to himself: "I may as well let him go!" So he said to the acorn: "Roll on behind then!" But that was a strange rolling, for the acorn leaped to its feet and frisked along in front of them all. And they came into a thick forest, a forest most drear and dreadful, and in the forest stood a lonely little hut—oh! so lonely. There was no fire burning in the stove, and there stood there a frumenty-pottage for six. The acorn, who knew what he was about, immediately leaped into the pottage, the little cord stretched itself out on the threshold, the grandfather placed the little water-mill on the bench, the drake sat upon the stove, and the grandfather himself stood in the corner. Suddenly he heard a crashing and a trembling in the wood, and Verlioka came along on one leg, in a wooden boot, leaning on his crutch, and smiling from ear to ear. Verlioka came up to the hut, threw down some firewood on the floor, and began to light the fire in the stove. But the acorn who was sitting in the pottage fell a-singing,

> *"Pee, pee, pee!*
> *To beat Verlioka come we!"*

Verlioka flew into a rage and seized the pot by the handle, but the handle broke, and all the pottage was scattered over the floor, and the acorn leaped out of the pot and flipped Verlioka in his one eye so that it was put out entirely. Verlioka fell a-shrieking, fought about the air with his arms, and would have made for the door; but where was the door? He could not see it! Then the little cord wound itself about his legs and he fell on the threshold, and the little water-mill on the top of him off the bench. Then the grandfather rushed out of the corner and pitched into him with his iron crutch, and the drake on the top of the stove screeched with all its might: "Tak, tak, tak! Pitch into him! pitch into him!" Neither his wrath nor his strength was of any good to Verlioka. The grandfather beat him to death with his iron crutch, and after that destroyed his hut and laid bare the dungeon beneath it, and out of the dungeon he drew his grandchildren, and dragged all Verlioka's riches home to his old woman.

And so he lived and prospered with his old woman and his grandchildren, and plucked and ate his peas in peace and quietness. So there's a tale for you—and I deserve a cake or two also.

The Lord of Death

INDIA

There was a road, and everyone who traveled on it died. Some people said they were killed by a snake, others said by a scorpion, but somehow they all died.

Once a very old man was traveling along the road. When he got tired, he sat down on a stone, and suddenly he saw in front of him a huge scorpion. It was as big as a rooster, and even as he was looking at it, it changed into a snake and glided away. Wonderstruck, he decided to follow it at a little distance and find out what it really was.

The snake glided here and there, day and night, and behind it followed the old man like a shadow. Once it went into an inn and killed several travelers; another time it slid into the palace and killed the king himself. It crept up the waterspout to the queen's quarters and killed her youngest daughter. So it passed on, and wherever it went there was soon the sound of weeping and wailing, and the old man followed it, silent as a shadow.

The road suddenly turned into a broad, deep river, on the banks of which sat some poor travelers who longed to cross over but had no money to pay the ferryman. Then the snake changed into a handsome buffalo, with a brass necklace and bells around its neck, and stood by the brink of the stream. When the travelers saw this, they said, "This beast is going to swim to its home across the river. Let's get on its back and hold on to its tail, and we too can get to the other side."

So they climbed on its back, and the buffalo swam into the river. But when it reached the middle, where the river was deepest, it began to kick and roll until they all tumbled off, or let go, and were all drowned.

When the old man, who had crossed the river in a boat, reached the other side, the buffalo had disappeared, and in its stead stood a beautiful ox. Seeing this handsome creature wandering about, without any owner in sight, a peasant coveted it and lured it to his home. It was quite gentle, and allowed him to tie it up with his other cattle. But in the dead of night it changed into a snake, bit all the flocks and herds, killed all the sleeping folk, and crept away. But behind it, the old man still followed, silent as a shadow.

Soon they came to another river, where the snake changed itself into the likeness of a beautiful young woman covered with jewels. After a while, two brothers, both of them soldiers, came that way, and as they came towards her, she began to weep bitterly.

"What is the matter?" asked the brothers. "And why are you, a young and beautiful woman, sitting here alone?"

Then the snake woman answered, "My husband was taking me home. We were waiting for the ferry. He went to wash his face, slipped on a stone, fell into the river, and was drowned. Now I have no one. My relatives are far away."

"You've nothing to be afraid of," said the elder of the two brothers, who was much taken with her beauty. "Come with me and I will marry you and look after you."

"On two conditions," answered the woman. "You must never ask me to do any household work. And you must give me whatever I ask."

"I'll obey you like a slave!" said the young man.

"Then go to that well and get me a cup of water. Your brother will stay here with me," said the woman.

But as soon as the elder brother's back was turned, she said to the younger, "Let's leave before he comes back. I love you. I sent your brother away to get rid of him."

"No, no," said the young man. "You promised to be his wife. You are like a sister to me."

At this the woman was furious. She began to weep and wail when she saw the elder brother returning with the water. She cried out to him, "This brother of yours is an evil man. He asked me to run away with him and leave you here!"

Before the younger could say a word, the elder had drawn his sword and they began to fight. They fought all day long and by evening they lay dead on the banks of the river. Then the woman took the form of a snake once more, and the old man followed it, silent as a shadow.

At last the snake changed into an old white-bearded man. When the old man who was following it saw another ancient like himself, he took courage, went closer, and asked, "Who and what are you?"

Then the old white-bearded man smiled and answered, "Some people call me the Lord of Death, because I go about bringing death to the world."

"Give me death!" pleaded the other. "I've followed you for days and watched your ways. And I'm sick at heart."

But the Lord of Death shook his head and said, "Oh no, not yet. I give only to those whose time has come. You've sixty more years to go!"

Then the old white-bearded man vanished. But was he really the Lord of Death or a devil? Who can tell?

The Man Who Lodged with Serpents

HUNGARY

One day an old man set forth to his vineyard. On his way there he had to pass a pit—a very deep pit, indeed. This was in wintertime when there was a sharp frost and everything was frozen. When he reached the vineyard, the snow began to fall. It came down in big flakes, as big as your sandals, and it became thicker and thicker as it went on snowing. The man braced himself with a glass or two of wine and decided to wait until the snow stopped falling so that he could go back home. In his shoulderbag he put three bottles of wine which he wanted to take home to his folks. Meanwhile it began to grow dark. The snow reached now to his knees, so he did not want to wait any longer and started to make his way homeward. He had to pass by the edge of the pit, but missing his step on the untrodden snow, he slipped right into the pit. Perhaps he had had a drop too much of the wine; and we must remember that he was not a young man either, and that the snow was slippery and the pit had a sloping wall. No matter how he tried, he went deeper and deeper down into the hole instead of getting out of it. When he got to the bottom, he felt as if he had come to a nice warm place. He looked around and found himself in a small room. Curled up in one corner there was a big snake, as thick as a man's body. There was another snake, just as thick and big as the first one, curled up in the opposite corner. In front of each snake there was a big stone, but it was not really stone, it was salt, a big chunk of rock salt. For a while the man gazed at the snakes, and the snakes stared back at him. He was in a blue funk, then and there, but he could not get out of the pit as the walls were too steep for him to climb.

After he had been there for two days, one of the snakes wriggled up close to him. It did not want to do him any harm, it even rubbed itself against his side. The man took heart at this and when the snake began licking the salt as if it wanted to encourage him to follow its example, the man took a lick at it too. He was hungry, and the snakes seemed to expect him to, so he fed himself on the salt; and as long as the three bottles lasted, he took a good swig at them. As he was not able to get out of the pit, and as he had nothing else to eat, he lived on the salt for the whole winter.

His folks at home made a wide search for him, here and there, but all in vain. There was no trace of him. The short of it was that they could not find him. So what! He was gone for good. And that was that. For a few years they still hoped for his return, but as he did not come back they divided his land and whatever he possessed among themselves. After all, they had lost their father; he had vanished into thin air, and there was nothing to do about it.

One day a *garabonciás*, a magic maker, came to the pit to have a look at his snakes. They belonged to him, and he wanted to use them for horses. The pit the old man had fallen into was the very one the *garabonciás* used to rear his snakes. But this time he did not find them strong enough. "You'll have to stay here for another seven years," he said. "And after that perhaps I will find you good enough." Hearing this, the man implored the *garabonciás* to take him out of the pit. But he refused. "Here you stay. This is a good place for you. After seven years you can leave with the snakes. Until then you can give me a hand with these beasts."

So the man had to spend seven years in the pit. Seven years after the day of his first visit, the *garabonciás* came again. This time he brought a pair of bridles. The heads of the snakes were like the heads of horses, so the *garabonciás* had brought two red bridles and two matching reins for them. One bridle and one rein he gave to the man; one bridle and one rein he kept for himself. "Now take this bridle and put it on this snake here, and I am going to bridle the other snake myself," he said to the man, "but take care that you do not miss at the first try when you fix the curb bit into its mouth, or you are a dead man. The beasts will tear you to pieces. But if you are clever enough when you fix the bit, no harm will come to you. When you have done that, you can jump on its back and it will fly out with you from this pit. That's your only chance of ever getting out of this hole."

So it happened. The man fixed the bit and the rein on to one snake, and the *garabonciás* did the same with his own. Riding their snakes, they were soon carried out of the pit. Then the old man got off the snake's back and gave the reins to the *garabonciás*. And off went the *garabonciás* and his two snakes. But all along their way they were followed by a terrific storm with hail which destroyed crops and fruit and all.

So after seven years, the old man got out of the pit. Seven years, you know, is quite a long time, and there were all sorts of changes so that the place seemed just a bit strange to the man, but he still remembered the way to his village and soon he was bound for home.

When he arrived in the village, they recognized him at once in spite of the fact that his beard had grown quite white. But superstition still had a strong hold on people, and they were afraid of him and kept out of his way. He called after them, "Do not be afraid of me. I am a living creature"; but they were scared of him. When he came to his own place, he found it changed too. His sons had divided among themselves what once belonged to him, and nothing was the same as when he had seen it last. Even his own children fled from the house when they caught sight of him. They feared that he had come back to right some wrong which they might have done. So it was only after some time that he was able to make them stop and listen to him. "Don't be afraid of me. I fell into a pit. I can show you which one. And that is where I have been all that time."

So his sons lost their fear and asked their father to live with them. But he had not long to live. He had lived too long on air spoiled by natural gas during the seven years he was kept in the pit. He was no longer able to live on fresh air. It made him die.

Kwatee and the Monster in Lake Quinault

NATIVE AMERICAN/QUINAULT

When Kwatee, the Changer, was an old man, he traveled down the coast until he came to Lake Quinault. A monster lived in Lake Quinault, a monster so big that it could swallow a cedar canoe. As Kwatee arrived at the lake, he saw his brother out in a canoe and called to him.

But at that very moment the monster stuck his head out of the water, opened his huge mouth, and swallowed the canoe, with Kwatee's brother in it.

Kwatee set to work at once to save his brother. He gathered all the big rocks around the lake and heated them. Then with a pair of tongs he tossed the hot rocks into the lake. When the water was boiling hot, the monster floated on the surface of the lake, dead.

Kwatee then made a sharp knife of mussel shells. He planned to cut the monster open, so that his brother might get out. As he cut, he kept singing, "Don't be afraid, little brother. I will soon set you free."

But when the monster was cut open, the brother did not jump out. Inside the monster's stomach he had been changed into a hermit crab. Kwatee's brother was the father of all hermit crabs in the world today.

Kwatee was so angry that he hurled his tongs out into the ocean and changed them into stone. The tongs were open, and the handle was pointing up. You can see them today—the split rocks near the village of Tahola at the mouth of the Quinault River.

Kwatee continued his journey for a little while longer. Then, feeling old and tired, he knew that he had made all the changes he could make to help the new people who were to come. He climbed upon a rock that overlooks the ocean and sat watching the setting sun. When the copper ball had disappeared into the water, Kwatee pulled his blanket over his face and turned himself into stone.

You can see him today, south of the village of Tahola, sitting on a rock near where Point Grenville juts out into the sea.

Lump Off, Lump On

JAPAN

An old man had a big lump on the right side of his face, as big as a big tangerine. It made him so ugly that he avoided other people and instead worked alone in the mountains cutting wood. Once he got caught in an awful storm and had to stay in the mountains overnight.

No one else was around. He hid, wide awake and terrified, in a hollow tree. Feeling as lonely as he did, he breathed a sigh of relief when he heard other people coming. Then he peeked outside. The crowd, a hundred strong, was a horrible sight. Some in it were red dressed in green, some were black with a red loincloth, some had one eye or no mouth, and most were just indescribable. They built a fire as bright as the sun and made a circle round it, right in front of the old man's tree. He was frightened nearly out of his wits.

One monster, apparently the chief, sat down by the fire in the place of honor, and the rest sat in twin rows to his right and left. Next, they all began drinking and carrying on the way people do. As the wine jar went round and round, the chief got awfully drunk. When a young monster with a tray made his way slowly up to the chief, mumbling something or other, the chief burst out laughing and waved his cup. They really were just like people! The young monster danced, and when he had finished another began. Each one took his turn, right on up to the senior monsters, and if some danced badly others danced well. The old man could hardly believe his eyes.

"This is the most fun we've ever had!" the chief declared. "Now let's have something really special!"

Goodness knows what got into the old man then—perhaps some god or buddha put him up to it—but he suddenly wanted to get out there and dance. At first he checked himself, but the monsters had a fine rhythm going and the temptation was just too much. Out he burst from his hollow tree, with his hat down over his nose and an axe dangling from his belt, right before the chief.

The monsters jumped up. "What's this?" they cried. The old man leaped high and squatted low, he twisted and wriggled all around with hoots and shouts of "Ei!" and "Ho!" till everyone burst out laughing.

"We've been having these parties for years," chuckled the chief, "but no one like *you* has ever joined us! Be here every time from now on!"

"Say no more!" cried the old man. "I will! But it was all so sudden this time that I forgot how to end my dance right. If you liked me tonight, just wait till you see me dance properly!"

"You were wonderful!" the chief insisted. "Make sure you come again!"

One of the chief's lieutenants was not quite convinced. "The old fellow's full of promises," he objected, "but I'm not so sure he *will* be back. We'd better keep something of his as security."

That sounded like a good idea. The chief asked what they should take.

There was a buzz of voices. "What about the lump on his face?" the lieutenant suggested. "A lump's good luck and he'll miss it."

"Oh please," the old fellow begged, "take my eyes or my nose, but not my lump! I've had it for years! You're too cruel!"

"Aha!" said the lieutenant. "You see? That's what we need!"

A monster stepped up to the old man and twisted the

lump off painlessly. "Be sure you're at our next party!" he warned.

Soon it was dawn and the birds were singing. The monsters went away. The old man felt his face and found that the lump he had had for so long was gone. He forgot all about cutting wood and hurried home to his astonished wife.

Now, the old man next door had a lump on the *left* side of his face, and when he saw his neighbor's was gone he wanted to know how the old fellow had done it. "What doctor did you go to?" he asked. "Please tell me! I can't stand mine!"

"It wasn't a doctor, it was a monster."

"Well, either way, I'll just do whatever you did. So what did you do?"

The first old man told his story and the second listened carefully. He went to hide in the hollow tree, and sure enough the monsters came. They sat in a ring, drank and carried on, and roared, "Where's that old man?"

The second old man was terribly afraid but he staggered out anyway. "Hurray!" the monsters shouted. "Here he is!"

"All right!" said the chief. "Now, dance!"

He danced, but his faltering steps had nothing in common with his neighbor's gleeful zest.

"That was terrible," the chief grumbled. "Give him back his lump!"

Up stepped a junior monster. "Here's your lump back," he said, and stuck it on the other side. The old man had gotten himself two lumps instead of one.

Siksruk, the Witch-Doctor

ESKIMO

Once, long ago, the small son of a very rich Eskimo chief disappeared and nobody could find him. The village was full of witch-doctors, all of whom claimed great powers, but try as they might not one of them could find a trace of the boy. The parents of the boy were grief-stricken, for he was their only child.

When hope that he might yet be found was almost abandoned, an old man named Siksruk came to the father.

"I do not claim to be a real witch-doctor," said the modest Siksruk, "yet I might be able to find your boy."

"If you find him I will give you half of my wealth," said the anxious chief, grasping at the last straw.

Thereupon the old man took his drum and as he beat it he chanted a strange song. When he finished, he sat up smiling and said, "I think perhaps the animals took that boy. Maybe I can find him, though. Tell the people to gather some food for a trip and I will go tomorrow."

The chief saw that Siksruk was properly outfitted and the old man started off across the tundra alone. On and on he went towards the hills until at length he came to a very small igloo, half-buried in the ground. Noiselessly he crept to the tiny window and peeped in. Down below he saw a strange-looking man and woman, and between them sat the chief's small son.

Just as he took his first look the man down below said, "Those two old women are bad women." Then without looking up he continued, "You might as well come in. We know who you are."

Siksruk wondered how the old man had seen him but got down from his perch by the window and went in the door. But much to his surprise he found the room vacant. He searched for another door and found none, but in the floor he saw another tiny window. Looking down through this window he saw another room below him, and in it sat two old women, no doubt the ones the man was talking about.

So Siksruk changed himself into a hair and dropped lightly to the floor between the two old women. No sooner had the hair lit than the old women pointed to it and exclaimed, "Oh, we know who you are!" The witch-doctor then assumed his own form and engaged the two women in conversation.

"That man up there," said Siksruk, "just said you women are no good." At that both women flew into a rage. "If you will show me where he is now," continued the crafty Siksruk, "I will pay you with something that I have."

The old women agreed to help Siksruk and led him to a secret door that opened into the room wherein sat the man, woman and the chief's lost son. When Siksruk entered, the man looked surprised to see him and then beckoned him to sit down. "I will sing for you," said the strange man and immediately began to chant a weird song. But as he sang the magic song, things began to change. The ceiling of the igloo became open sky and in it hundreds of birds were flying. When the song was finished everything changed back and

Siksruk said, "That was very good singing. Now I'll sing for you." He began to chant slowly at first, then faster and louder and wilder. "Stop singing!" shouted the man, who was becoming alarmed. "That is enough!"

"No, I'll finish my song first," said Siksruk and continued, wilder than ever. All at once he dropped his voice to a whisper and said to the woman, "Go look out of your stormshed door." Then he resumed his song.

The frightened woman went out quickly and returned at once, crying bitterly. "The sea is rolling right before our door!" wept the terrified woman. The man leapt up and ran to the door. The sea was coming in! He shut the door and turned to Siksruk pale and trembling.

"Now may I have the boy?" asked Siksruk.

"Yes!" shouted the man and woman together. "Save us from the sea and you may take him!"

So Siksruk ended his song and the sea receded. Then, taking the chief's boy, he left the igloo and started back to the village.

Great was the rejoicing when he entered with the long-lost boy. The chief was overjoyed to have him back again and true to his promise gave Siksruk half his wealth, which included black whalebone and many spotted deerskins.

Old Roaney

UNITED STATES

One time there was an old man lived on yonder side of the mountain. He was an awful hand to hunt, hunted all the time, never *had* follered nothin' but huntin'. Him and his old woman they lived mostly on wild meat. 'Course they had to buy a little meal and coffee and sech. And this was back in old times when it was pretty thin-settled in here, and the settle-ment (that's where the store was at), hit was plumb the other side of the mountain.

Well, one cold winter mornin' the old lady raised up from where she was a-cookin' in the fireplace, says, "Old man, we done run plumb out of salt. I told you last week that salt-gourd was rattlin' mighty holler. And besides that, there hain't a scrap of meal left, and I cooked up the very last ground of coffee for your breakfast this mornin', and we're low on sugar, and I scraped on the bottom of the flour barr'l last night when I made up your biscuits. You done let us run out of rations. Now you saddle your old pack-mare and git on over that mountain or we'll be eatin' nothin' but unsalted meat."

"Well," says the old man, "I'll be goin' out in a day or two, I reckon. Hit's a-snowin' pretty bad right now."

"You git Old Roaney and fetch us in some rations *today*, old man. You can eat wild meat with no salt and no bread if you want, but I ain't a-goin' to stand for no sech a thing. Git out of here now and go on to the store like I tell ye."

"Well," he says, "I'll go directly."

That old man he wasn't even studyin' about makin' ar' trip out to the settle-ment, cold as it was: but when he went to fill up his powder horn, his last keg of powder had jest a little bitty dribble in it. "Blame!" he says, "I can't fetch in much game with that." He *had* to go to the store now.

So he pulled his old coonskin hat down over his ears, opened the door-shutter, hollered "Roaney!," whistled a couple of times. Old Roaney nickered and directly here she come a-trompin' through the snow. She 'uz an awful good old mare. Come on to the house and stood there to see what did the old man want. So he give her a peck of oats. (Only crop the old man ever did raise. Had him a little deadened patch of newground in the bottoms where he put in a few oats ever' year for his old mare. He didn't like farmin'; didn't like to foller *nothin'* but huntin' and a little fishin' ever' now and then.) So he took the saddle off the wall and throwed hit on Old Roaney. Waited for her to git done mommickin' her oats. Then he bridled her and tied on a few furs he had saved up, jumped in the saddle and hunkered down in his coat collar, and give Old Roaney her head. She 'uz a good old mare. She knowed it was about time to go out and pack in some rations and ammunition. So she took the old man right on over the mountain and on down to the settle-ment. Hit was a right far piece.

So when Old Roaney fin'lly stopped, the old man knowed she was at the store. Stuck his head up out of his old coat, grabbed up his bundle of furs and jumped off and run on in, throwed the furs down on the counter and started in tradin'. Well, he got eight bushels of meal and eight big tins of bakin' sody, a two-hundred-pound sack of tree sugar, hundred pounds of green coffee (that was back in old times when you had to roast it and grind it at home), three two-bushel pokes of wheat-flour, fifty-pound poke of salt, twelve fifty-pound kegs of powder, several dozen bars of lead (had to mold your own bullets back then; muzzle-loadin' hog-rifles was all they had to shoot with), got himself twenty-four dozen twists of tobacco, and several little ar-ticles for his wife. Took all that out and packed it on his old mare. Crawled up in the saddle, says, "Git-up, Roaney." And Old Roaney started on off toward the mountain.

Now, the old man had him a few balls left in his shot-pouch, and he'd done tapped the bung in one of them kegs of powder and filled up his powder horn, so he had his gun ready to fire. (The old folks they *al*-ways kept their old hog-rifles ready-loaded to shoot.) And when they got on up in the mountain he looked out and seen a big buck deer standin' up the slope a little piece. Upped with his rifle-gun . . . BAM! . . . and down come the deer. Went and got it, dragged it out in the trail, skinned him a strop of rawhide off one of its legs, tied its feet together, heaved it up and hung it on the saddle horn. Got back in the saddle and on they went. Looked out before him directly and here come a great big old black bear a-shummickin' right down the middle of the trail. "If I can jest git you now, your fat'll season my buck." (Well, the old folks *always* kept their long-rifles ready-loaded.) So he upped with the muzzle, squeezed the trigger, and at the crack of the gun down come the bear. Hit 'uz a big 'un too. The old man dragged it down on the uphill side of the trail, prized it up on a log was layin' there about level with the old mare's back, got its feet tied up, pulled Old Roaney over to that log and hooked the bear's feet over the saddle-horn. Got back in the saddle—"Git-up, Roaney"—and Old Roaney started easin' away from that log. Now, when that bear's weight pulled off the log and struck Old Roaney she stopped and turned her head and looked back at the old man. But she was an awful good old mare: she stretched out and shifted her fore feet, put her old head down and shifted her hind feet, and picked her way up the mountain.

When they got up in the gap the old man thought he 'uld let her blow a spell 'fore he started down. And while he was a-waitin' he heard a dove moanin' right close; looked out before him and seen it sittin' on a dead limb right over the trail. Well, he thought he'd take his old woman a little bait of fresh bird-meat for her supper. So he upped with his old rifle-gun (the old folks never did fail to keep their guns ready-loaded), and he took that dove right in the head. It fell and caught in the bresh 'side the trail, so directly he pulled on over there and reached down out the saddle to pick it up. And—don't you know!—time he took holt on that dove, little as it was, Old Roaney scooched down and her back give away. Still, she 'uz an awful good old mare. She always done the best she could: she kept her head up and her rump up, but her old belly swagged on the ground. So the old man jumped off of her, seen the shape she was in, says, "Now I declare! I believe Old Roaney's back's done gone and broke. Now, what'n the nation will I do?"

Well, he unloaded her but she still couldn't heave herself off'n the ground; so the old man jest knowed her back was broke, and he got to studyin' what to do. So he split Old

Roaney down the forehead, and cut her around the hocks, and then he slipped up behind her with a two-handed bresh—and come at her hollerin' and swarped her good—and it scared her so she jumped right out of her skin.

So then the old man took Old Roaney's skin and stretched it out on the ground, put them rations and all that plunder in it, and the deer and the bear and the dove, and tied the four legs across, got his head up through it where he'd left it tied jest right, took holt on a little dogwood tree and pulled up, swung that load around on his back and put out down the mountain.

Well, he got in home, jerked open the door-shutter, and went on in the house. Now, he'd forgot his pipe when he went out and he was wantin' a smoke awful bad. So he walked over to the fireplace, got his old cob pipe down off the fireboard, crumbled some tobacco in it, scooped him up a coal of fire and got it lit. Started in walkin' the floor, a-smokin' and a-worryin' about his old pack-mare. He thought the world of Old Roaney. Well, he tromped backerds and forrads a spell, a-smokin' and a-worryin', and directly his old woman raised up, looked at him, says, "Old man, why in the nation don't you lay that pack down and go get washed for supper?"

So the old man he slung his pack off on the floor and untied it. Piled them rations in one corner, put his powder in a good dry place, throwed the bars of lead down one side the hearthrock, laid his tobacco on one end of the fireboard and his wife's stuff on the other, skun out the deer and the bear and took the meat on out and hung it up, picked and cleaned that dove and handed it to his old lady. Then he took the deer-skin and the bear-skin and Old Roaney's hide and throwed them down behind the door where he kept all his skins and sech. So him and the old woman they eat supper and went on to bed.

Well, 'way up in the night the old lady woke up, punched her old man, says, "Get up, old man, and see what that is pawin' at the door. Sounds like Old Roaney, sure's the world!"

"Old Roaney—the nation! Old Roaney's up there on top of the mountain with her back broke and no hide on her. Go on back to sleep, old woman."

The old lady she tried to go to sleep but she couldn't. And directly she heard it again: pawin', pawin'. So she gouged the old man with her elbow, says, "Old man, you get up now and go see what that is. Sounds pint blank like Old Roaney, the way she does everwhen you forget to feed her and she comes a-pawin' at the door after ye."

"I done told ye, old woman! Old Roaney's up there on the mountain with her back broke plumb in two and her hide a-layin' there behind the door. Now, you hush up and quit botherin' me."

So the old man he rolled over and commenced snorin'; but the old lady couldn't get to sleep and couldn't get to sleep, and then she heard it again—pawin', pawin', pawin' like it 'uld break down the doorstep; and that time it nickered. So she raised up and jerked the covers off the old man, set in to punchin' him and shakin' him till she got him woke up, says, "Now you get right out of this bed, old man, and go see what that is. I heard it nicker jest now, and I tell ye hit *is* Old Roaney. You git your britches on and go yonder and open that door, or I'll not give ye no more peace the rest of this night."

"Old woman, you're crazy as a betsy-bug! Hit's a heifer plunderin' around out there, or some other brute done broke loose from somewhere. Well, jest to pacify ye, I'll have to show you hit ain't old Roaney."

So the old man he crawled out. Put a chunk of lightwood on the fire and when it flared up he went and opened the door; and Old Roaney stuck her head in the house. There she was, the cold snow a-foggin' and a-pilin' down on her, and her jest a-shakin' and a-shiverin' with no hide to her back. So the old man he reached down behind the door right quick to get her skin and put it back on her. Got out there tryin' to get it stretched out to cover her and it didn't seem to go jest right. Well, he 'lowed he'd have to tie it on, but he didn't have no hickory bark twists handy, so he reached over close to the house where he knowed some blackberry bushes was at, broke him off a handful and wrenched 'em and twisted 'em till he'd fixed him up a withe. Tied the skin on his old mare with that withe. Went on back and jumped in the bed. Old Roaney didn't bother 'em no more, and him and the old woman slept right on.

Well, the next mornin' when it got daylight enough the old man looked out to see about his old pack-mare—and he seen what a bobble he'd made. He'd killed a big buck sheep a couple of days before, and instead of gettin' Old Roaney's hide he had grabbed up that sheep-skin and tied hit on her. He went out and tried to pull it off, and—don't you know!—hit had done took root and wouldn't come. So he jest left it, and hit growed right on. Covered her bodaciously all over in jest a very few weeks. Growed down her legs and underneath her, wool patches on her head, and the biggest sheep-tail you ever seen a-hangin' down behind. And they tell me the old man sheared her twicet a year. Got more wool off Old Roaney than forty head of sheep. Peart too, but she *was* sorty swaybacked the rest of her days.

And I have heard it told how that blackberry withe took root around her like a bellyband. And the old woman never did have to go out in the bresh no more after her black-berries. When blackberry time come she 'uld jest call Old Roaney and pick blackberries off her sides—got enough to make several pies, ever' pickin'. But I'll jest tell ye now. I never did really believe *that* part of the tale.

The Old Woman and
the Rice Cakes

JAPAN

Long ago, in Japan, there was a cheerful old woman who lived alone in a small house halfway up a steep hill. She had a few chickens and a pig, but very little else. Quite often she had only one meal a day.

One evening she had just finished making a small bowl of round rice cakes for her dinner, when the bowl slipped and the rice cakes fell to the floor. To her dismay, they rolled right out the doorway. The old woman ran after them.

Once outside, the rice cakes rolled down the steep hill, bouncing over rocks, going faster and faster. The woman scurried down the hill behind them, but she could not catch up with them until they came to rest at the very bottom, near a large slab of rock.

Just as the woman bent over to pick up her rice cakes, a long, blue, scaly arm with a three-fingered, clawlike hand reached out from behind the rock and snatched them from her.

"That's my dinner!" she cried. She peered behind the rock slab, and seeing a small opening, in she went right after her rice cakes.

She found herself in a narrow tunnel. Ahead of her was a large, shambling creature hurrying away.

"Sir!" she called loudly, trotting after him. "My dinner! You've taken my dinner!" But the creature went right on, with the woman close behind him, until they reached a large cave.

The old woman stopped short in surprise. In the cave were several more large creatures. They had horns on their heads, wide mouths that stretched from ear to ear, and three red, staring eyes. She realized she was in a den of Oni, ogres who lived under the ground and came forth only at night. The Japanese Oni, like trolls and demons in other parts of the world, are always bent on evil mischief.

She was, however, more angry than frightened, for the Oni had greedily shared her rice cakes among themselves and gulped them down.

"You're no better than thieves!" she cried. "You've eaten my rice cakes and now I have no dinner!"

But they only sat licking their large, clawlike hands, staring at her so hungrily that she wondered if they were going to eat her next.

Then one of them said, "Did you make the rice cakes?"

"Yes, I did," retorted the old woman. "I make very tasty rice cakes, if I do say so myself."

"Come along, then, and make more!" said he, and he clumped away through a maze of tunnels and caves. The old woman followed him, for she was by now quite hungry and she thought it only fair that the ogres should give her dinner.

But by the time they arrived at the cave full of huge round cooking pots, she realized she was hopelessly lost. She doubted she could ever find the small hole in the rock where she came in.

The Oni dropped a few grains of rice into a large pot of water.

"That will never make enough rice cakes!" she said crossly.

"Of course it will, stupid creature," he scowled. He picked up a flat wooden stirrer. "Put this into the pot and start stirring."

The woman did as she was told. At once the few grains of rice increased until almost the whole pot was filled. So the old woman made the ogres a huge pile of rice cakes—taking care to eat some herself first, before handing them over.

"I'll be going home now," she announced firmly, "if you'll show me the way back to the entrance."

"Oh, no," growled the Oni. "You will stay here and cook for us."

This did not suit the little old woman at all, but as she looked at the large monsters crowded about, licking their claws, she thought she had better not say so.

Nevertheless, while the woman worked to make piles of rice cakes for the hungry Oni, she thought and thought about how to escape. She soon discovered that the source of the water for cooking the rice was a stream nearby, flowing along between the rock caverns. She thought this must be the same stream that flowed out of the bottom of the hill below her home. Farther on, it became a river, and the people of the village fished from its banks.

But there was no boat to be seen.

"The Oni would not have a boat," thought the old woman. "It's well known the wicked creatures cannot go over water!"

Without a boat, how could she escape? She thought of this as she cooked and stirred—until she saw that one of the large round pots might do very well. They were as big as she was.

The Oni, being night creatures, slept during the day, sprawled in the many caves under the hill. The next day, as soon as they were all asleep, she put the magic stirring paddle in a huge pot and dragged the pot down to the stream.

It floated very nicely, so she hopped in and started to paddle. But the grating sound of the pot being dragged to the stream had wakened a number of Oni nearby. Suddenly they appeared on the side of the stream, shouting in rage.

The old woman paddled faster and faster. Ahead she could see a patch of sunlight where the stream made its way out into the world.

But the stream began to shrink, and grew smaller and smaller. Then she saw that the Oni were drinking up the water, swelling up like monstrous balloons as they sucked in the stream. Rocks and stones began to show in the bed of the stream. The huge pot ground to a halt. All around her, stranded fish flopped about helplessly on the stones.

It seemed the ogres could soon walk across the gravel to seize her. Quick as a wink, the old woman picked up the fish and tossed them, one after another, to the ogres on the banks.

"Have some fish stew!" she called.

The Oni caught the fish in their claws—and because they were always hungry, they opened their wide mouths to gulp down the fish. As soon as they did this, the water rushed out of their mouths again, back into the stream—which, of course, was just what the old woman had hoped would happen.

The round pot floated free, and off the old woman paddled, out of the hill and into broad daylight.

When she had floated down the stream to a safe distance, she paddled over to the nearest bank. Hopping ashore, she pushed the big pot back into the water to drift farther downstream. This, she thought, would mislead the Oni if they should come looking for her. But she kept the magic stirrer with her and climbed safely back up the hill to her house.

The old woman never went hungry again, for with the magic stirrer she was able to make as many rice cakes as she could eat—and she had enough left over to share with her neighbors.

But if any rice cakes fell to the floor and rolled away down the hill, she never went after them.

"Let the Oni have them," she'd say cheerfully. And so, with her chickens, her pig, and plenty of rice for her dinner, she lived very happily the rest of her days.

The Poor Countryman
and the Greedy Hag

POLAND

There was once a poor old man living in a forest, who made a skimpy livelihood by collecting twigs that he sold for kindling, and although he'd worked hard all his life he had nothing to show for it in the end. But one day, as he was cutting down a tree, he heard a cry for help and saw a man, his wagon and his horses sinking in a quagmire. He ran at once to help, pulled them all to safety on firm soil, and the rescued man told him that he could have anything he wanted.

"I am a great magician," the man said. "Whatever you want is yours for the asking."

The poor countryman had never had anything of value, so he didn't know what to ask for now that his chance had come, but while he stood there and scratched his head, wondering what to say, the magician gave him a big ram with a golden fleece.

"Whenever you shake this ram," he told the countryman, "gold ducats will fall out of his fleece."

The countryman said his thanks, took the ram to his poor hut in the forest and gave him a good shake, and at once gold coins spilled out of the ram's fleece.

His happiness, however, didn't last a month. Good fortune causes gossip, and gossip finds sharp ears, and it wasn't long before the story got to a certain old hag, said to be a witch, who lived near the forest. She made the countryman drunk one day, stole the magic ram, and put another in his place. The next day, needing another ducat, the countryman shook his ram again but no gold came flying from his fleece. The ram bleated and struggled to get away but not a penny appeared anywhere near him.

The poor old man went sadly to the quagmire, where he thought he might as well put an end to his life and be done with it, but the magician was waiting for him there and gave him a hen.

"Every time you want a golden egg," he said, "just ask this hen and she will lay it for you."

The countryman took the hen home but the old hag soon found out about her and made him drunk again. She stole the magic hen and put another in her place, and no matter how the poor old man asked this new hen for a golden egg she would never lay one. The witch got whatever golden eggs there were.

Sad once again, the poor countryman complained to the

magician, who gave him a magic tablecloth which spread itself with all and any food and drink that anyone might want.

"All that you have to do is say 'Tablecloth, tablecloth, spread thyself,'" the magician said, "and you will always have enough to eat."

Curious, the old man ordered the tablecloth to spread itself right there in the forest, and ate and drank so much that he fell asleep. But the hag was watching from behind a tree, and stole the tablecloth and slipped him another.

This time, however, the simple old man wasn't fooled so easily. He caught onto the old witch's tricks, went to the magician and asked him for something that would give the thieving hag a beating, and help him get back his ram, his hen and his tablecloth.

"All right, but this is the last thing I can do for you," the magician said and gave him a wicker basket with two thick cudgels lying on the bottom. "All that you have to do is cry out 'Fiddlesticks, fiddlesticks, come out of the basket,' and these two cudgels will jump right out of it and beat whoever you point to for as long as you want."

The countryman was delighted, thanked the kind magician and promised never to bother him again. Then he ran with his basket to the witch's house and knocked on her door.

"Who's there?" she shouted. "And what do you want?"

"It's me," the countryman said. "I've a magic basket that I want to show you."

She let him in at once and offered him a drink to put him to sleep, but he only shouted: "Fiddlesticks, fiddlesticks, come out of the basket," and pointed to the witch, and the two thick cudgels leaped out and started thrashing the hag without mercy.

She promised to give him back everything she'd stolen and begged his forgiveness, but the countryman let the cudgels go on with their work. She brought back the ram and the hen and the tablecloth, and all the golden coins and eggs that she had collected, but the countryman told the cudgels to keep pounding on her, because she was an evil old woman who had done a great deal of harm to many other people.

Then, finally, when she gave up the ghost, he said to his cudgels: "Fiddlesticks, fiddlesticks, back into my basket," and they jumped in at once.

Then, having a ram that spilled golden coins from his fleece each time he was shaken, a hen that laid a golden egg each time she was asked, a tablecloth that spread itself with a royal banquet any time he wished, and a pair of stout cudgels to thrash anyone who got in his way, he left the forest, went out into the world and joined the court of a certain king, where he became a great and powerful lord.

Later, when the king had a war, the clever countryman defeated all his enemies, married the king's daughter, and became the ruler of the entire country when the old king died.

St. David's Flood

ENGLAND

St. David's Flood is a name for the spring tide which in the old days brought Christian saints to Somerset. They came up river on St. David's Flood. Later on there was a fishing hamlet down by the shore, and one day all the men were out fishing and a little herd boy came running back to the village in terror to say that six Danish galleys were sailing along and would come up the river on St. David's Flood. Well, the women and the children scampered away to the nearby village of Uphill, which could give them some safety, and they could warn the farming folk there. But one old granny was down by the riverside gathering gladdon for thatching her cottage, and as the long ships sailed by she crouched down among the rushes and watched the Danes landing and scattering to plunder. They had tied up their boats and left them without even a guard. St. David's Flood had brought them up, the very flood that had carried the saints up in olden days, but it was turning now, it was not waiting for the pirates to finish their work.

When they had gone the old woman crept out from her hiding place and watched the tide. It runs out very quickly there, and she saw that it was on the turn. So she undid the mooring of each of the galleys, and then she stood and watched them jostling against each other, going down river and out into the Severn Sea. In the meantime the men of

Uphill had done their work well. They had ambushed the loaded pirates and driven them back toward their boats. But no boats were there, and not a pirate survived that bloody day. And that, they say, is why the village is called Bleadon.

The Staff of Elijah

JEWISH/MOLDAVIA

Long ago there was an old man who had once been very wealthy and had given charity willingly, but in his old age found himself impoverished. His neighbors remembered how generous he had been when he had been rich, so they often invited him to their homes and saw to it that his needs were met. It was this old man's custom to say twice the portion of the blessing over food which mentions Elijah: "May the Holy One send us Elijah the Prophet of blessed memory to bring us good tidings of redemption and salvation."

Once, when the Sabbath was over, the old man returned home, lit a candle, and was startled to find a Jew sitting on his bed. The old man was taken aback and said, "Who are you and where do you come from?" The stranger did not answer directly, but instead asked a question of his own, "Tell me, may I remain in your home for a few days?" And the old man replied, "Certainly you may stay, but what shall you eat, for I myself am dependent on the kindness of others?" The stranger said, "No matter," and remained as the guest of the old man. The two shared the old man's food, meager as it was, and the stranger accompanied the old man to synagogue.

After three days the stranger prepared to depart, but before he set out, he said to the old man, "Take my staff; it will help you. But someday you will have to return it to its place." Now these were strange words, which the old man did not understand. "Where is its place?" he asked. The stranger replied, "On Mount Carmel." This confused the old man even more, for Mount Carmel is in the Holy Land, far away from where the old man made his home. "Who are you?" he asked. And the stranger revealed that he was none other than Elijah the Prophet. Then the old man was afraid, overcome and happy all at once. He accepted the staff from Elijah with many thanks, and accompanied him to the door and saw him off. But when Elijah had taken but a few steps, he disappeared from the old man's sight, and the old man realized that this had truly been the prophet of old.

The next day the old man took the staff with him when he went to the market. While he was walking, the staff suddenly became stuck in a crack between the stones. The old man bent down to pull it out, and when he did he found several silver pieces in the shadow of the staff. What a blessing, he thought, for now he would be able to support himself again, and even have enough to give charity.

The old man soon discovered other powers of the staff. Once, when he had walked a long distance and was feeling faint, he sat down at the edge of the road and placed his staff so that only his feet touched it. At once he felt his strength renewed, as though he had become much younger. He was able to stand up easily and returned home full of life. After that he used the staff to revive himself whenever he began to feel the burden of his age, and his spirits always lifted at the very instant his feet touched the wondrous staff.

One night the old man was awakened by the sound of screams and cries. He ran outside with the staff in his hand to see what was happening, and discovered that the Jewish quarter had been invaded by a mob who were trying to set it afire. Suddenly the old man felt filled with a great strength, and he ran directly into the mob, swinging the staff. The other Jews marveled at the old man's courage and took heart, and they too joined the fight. In this way the rioters were quickly defeated, and never again did they dare to attack the Jewish quarter.

After this, the old man became a hero among the Jews of the town, and they decided to collect enough money for him to fulfill his lifelong wish of going to the Holy Land. So it was that he was able to make the journey after all, despite his age. After many months his ship arrived in Jaffa and the old man disembarked. His wish was to travel to the Wailing Wall in Jerusalem, but for some reason he could not fathom, he ended up in a wagon bound for Safed.

When the wagon was crossing Mount Carmel, one of its wheels broke off. There was nothing that could be done until the wheel was repaired, which would take some time. To pass the time the old man took a walk on the mountain, and along the way he spotted a tree from which a branch had been cut off. He came closer, and marveled that the wood of the tree was so similar to that of his staff. He raised up the staff against that place in the tree to compare it, and at the instant it touched the tree it fused to it and turned into one of its branches. While the old man watched in complete amazement, the branch began to bud and bear leaves, so that it soon resembled every other branch of that tree.

It was then that the old man recalled the words of Elijah, and understood that his mission was complete: the staff of Elijah had been returned to its place of origin. With a wonderful feeling the old man returned to the wagon just as the wheel was ready, and he continued on his journey. After visiting the holy city of Safed, he traveled to Jerusalem, as he had first intended, and before long reached the Wailing Wall. As he stood and prayed before the Wall, a wind gusted and carried a leaf to his feet. And when the old man bent down and picked it up, he somehow knew for certain it was a leaf from the tree from which his staff had been taken. The old man kept that leaf, and it remained green all the years of his life. And he lived many more years in the Holy Land, the happiest he had ever known.

The Magical Words

FINLAND

The aged and valiant Wainamoinen resolved to build himself a boat, a swift war-boat. He hewed the trees, he hewed the trunks of the pines and the firs, singing songs the while, chanting the runes that banish evil. And as he sang the smitten trees answered him, the fibres of the oak and of the fir and of the mountain pine yielded up their secrets in sounds that to other men seemed echoes only, but which to Wainamoinen's ears were syllables and words,—words wrung from the wood by enchantment.

Now only the keel remained to be wrought; the strong keel of the war-ship had yet to be fashioned. And Wainamoinen smote down a great oak, that he might carve and curve its body as keels are curved and carven. But the dying oak uttered its words of wood, its magical voice of warning, saying: "Never may I serve for the keel of thy boat, for the bottom of thy war-ship. Lo! the worms have made their crooked dwellings within my roots: yesterday the raven alighted upon my head; bloody was his back, bloody his crest, and blood lay clotting upon the blackness of his neck."

Therefore the ancient Wainamoinen left the oak, and sought among the mountain firs and the mountain pines for flawless keel-wood; and he found wood worthy of his war-boat, and he wrought the same into shape by the singing of magical songs.

For the words of enchantment by which shapes are shaped were known to him; by magical words he had wrought the hull, with magical words had formed the oars; and ribs and keel were by wizard song interlocked together. But to perfect the prow three words must be sung, three warlock words; and those three words Wainamoinen did not know, and his heart was troubled because he did not know them.

There was a shepherd dwelling among the hills, an ancient shepherd who had beheld ten times a hundred moons; and him Wainamoinen questioned concerning the three magical words.

But the ancient shepherd answered him dreamily: "Surely thou mayst find a hundred words, a thousand syllables of magical song, upon the heads of the swallows, upon the shoulders of the wild geese, upon the necks of the swans!"

Then the aged and valiant Wainamoinen went forth in search of the magical words. He slew the flying swallows by thousands; thousands of white geese he slew; thousands of snowy swans were stricken by his arrows. Yet he found no word written upon their heads, their shoulders, their necks, nor even so much as the beginning of a word. Then he thought unto himself: "Surely I may find a hundred words, a thousand syllables of song, under the tongues of the summer reindeer, within the ruddy mouth of the white squirrel."

And he went his way to seek the magical words. He strewed the vast plains with the bodies of slaughtered reindeer; he slew the white squirrels by thousands and tens of thousands. But he found no word beneath the tongue of the reindeer, no magical word in the mouth of the white squirrel, not even so much as the beginning of a word.

Yet again Wainamoinen thought to himself, saying: "Surely I may find a hundred magical words, a thousand syllables of song, in the dwelling of the Queen of Death, in the land of Tuonela, in the underground plains of Manala."

And he took his way unto the dwelling-place of Tuonela, to the moonless land of the dead, to the underground plains of Manala. Three days he journeyed thither with steps lighter than air; three days he journeyed as a shadow walking upon shadow.

And he came at last unto the banks of the sacred river, the sable shore of the black river, over which the spirits of the dead must pass; and he cried out to the children of Death: "O daughters of Tuoni, bring hither your bark! O children of Manala, bring hither your bark, that I may cross over the black river!"

But the daughters of Death, the children of Hell, cried out, saying: "The bark shall be taken over to thee only when thou shalt have told us how thou hast come to Manala, how thou hast reached Tuonela, the abode of Death, the domain of ghosts."

And Wainamoinen called out to them across the waters, saying: "Surely Tuoni himself hath conducted me hither; surely the Queen of Death hath driven me to Tuonela."

But the daughters of Tuonela waxed wroth; the virgins of Kalma were angry. And they answered: "We know the artifice of men; we perceive the lie within thy mouth. For surely thou livest! no wound hath slain thee; no woe hath consumed thee; no disaster hath destroyed thee; no grave hath been dug for thee. Who, therefore, hath brought thee alive to Manala?"

And Wainamoinen, answering, called out to them across the waters: "Iron surely hath brought me to the land of death; steel surely hath accompanied me unto Manala."

The daughters of Tuonela waxed wroth; the virgins of Kalma were angry. And they answered: "We know all artifices of men; we perceive the lie within thy mouth. Had iron brought thee to Tuonela, had steel accompanied thee unto Manala, thy garments would drip with blood. . . . Who brought thee to Manala?"

And Wainamoinen called out again to them across the

waters: "Fire hath brought me unto Manala; flame hath accompanied me to Tuonela."

The daughters of Tuonela waxed wroth; the virgins of Kalma were angry. And they cried out: "We know all artifices of men; we perceive the lie within thy mouth. Had fire brought thee to Manala, had flame accompanied thee to Tuonela, thy garments would be consumed by the fire, the glow of the flame would be upon thee. Who brought thee to Manala?"

And Wainamoinen yet again called out to them across the black river, saying: "Water hath brought me to Manala; water hath accompanied me to Tuonela."

The daughters of Tuonela waxed wroth; the virgins of Kalma were angry. And they answered, saying: "We know all the artifices of men; we perceive the lie within thy mouth. For there is no dripping of water from thy garments. Cease, therefore, to lie to us; for we know thou livest; we perceive that no wound hath slain thee, no woe consumed thee, no disaster hath crushed thy bones. Who brought thee to Manala? who guided thee to Tuonela?"

Then Wainamoinen called out to them across the river: "Surely I will now utter the truth. I have made me a boat by my art; I have wrought me a war-boat by magical song. With a song I shaped the hull; with a song I formed the keel; with a song I fashioned the oars. Yet three words are wanting to me, three magical words by which I may perfect the carven prow in its place; and I have come to Tuonela to find these three words; I have come to Manala to seek these three words of enchantment. Bring hither your bark, O children of Tuonela! bring hither your boat, O virgins of Kalma!"

So the daughters of Death came over the dark river in their black boat, and they rowed Wainamoinen to the further shore, to the waste of wandering ghosts; and they gave him to drink of what the dead drink, and to eat of what the dead devour. And Wainamoinen laid him down and slept, being weary with his mighty journey.

He slept and dreamed; but his garments slept not, his enchanted garments kept watch for him.

Now the daughter of Tuoni, the iron-fingered daughter of Death, seated herself in the darkness upon a great stone in the midst of the waters; and with iron fingers wove a net of iron thread, one thousand ells in length.

The sons of Tuoni, the sons of the Queen of Death, also seated themselves in the same darkness upon the same great stone in the midst of the same waters, and with their hookéd fingers, with their iron finger-nails, also wove a net of iron thread, a thousand ells in length.

And they cast their net into the river, across the river, that they might ensnare Wainamoinen, that they might entangle the magician, that they might prevent him from ever leaving the abyss of Manala, ever leaving the domain of Tuonela, so long as the golden moon should circle in heaven, even so long as the silver sun should light the world of men.

But the garments of Wainamoinen kept watch, the enchanted garments of the magician slept not. And Wainamoinen uttered a magical word, and changed himself into a stone; and the stone rolled into the black river.

And the stone became a viper of iron, and passed sinuously through the meshes of the nets, and through the river currents, and into the black reeds upon the black river's further bank.

So Wainamoinen passed from the kingdom of Tuoni, from the children of Death; but he had not found the magical words, nor so much as the part of a word.

Then thought Wainamoinen unto himself: "Surely I may find a hundred words, a thousand syllables of song, in the mouth of the earth-giant, in the entrails of the ancient Kalewa! Long is the way to his resting-place; one must travel awhile over the points of women's needles, and awhile upon the sharp edges of warriors' swords, and yet again awhile upon the sharp steel of the battle-axes of heroes."

And Wainamoinen went to the forge of his brother Ilmarinnen—Ilmarinnen, the Eternal Smith, who forged the vault of heaven, leaving no mark of the teeth of the pincers, no dent of the blows of the hammer—Ilmarinnen, who forged for men during the age of darkness a sun of silver and a moon of gold. And he cried out: "O Ilmarinnen, mighty brother, forge me shoes of iron, gloves of iron, a coat of iron! Forge me a staff of iron with a pith of steel, that I may wrest the magic words from the stomach of Kalewa, from the dead entrails of the earth-giant."

And Ilmarinnen forged them. Yet he said: "O brother Wainamoinen, the ancient Kalewa is dead; the grave of the earth-giant is deep. Thou mayst obtain no word from him,—not even the beginning of a word."

But Wainamoinen departed; Wainamoinen hastened over

the way strewn with the points of needles and the edges of swords and axe-heads of sharpest steel. He ran swiftly over them with shoes of iron; he tore them from his path with gloves of iron, until he reached the resting-place of Kalewa, the vast grave of the earth-giant.

For a thousand moons and more Kalewa had slept beneath the earth. The poplar-tree, the *haapa,* had taken root upon his shoulders; the white birch, the *koivu,* was growing from his temples; the elder tree, the *leppa,* was springing from his cheeks; and his beard had become overgrown with *pahju-*bark, with the bark of the drooping willow. The shadowy fir, the *oravikuusi,* was rooted in his forehead; the mountain-pine, the *havukonka,* was sprouting from his teeth; the dark spruce, the *petaja,* was springing from his feet.

But Wainamoinen tore the haapa from his shoulders, and the koivu from his temples, and the leppa from his cheeks, and the pahju-bark from his beard, and the oravikuusi from his forehead, and the havukonka from his teeth, and the petaja from his feet.

Then into the mouth of the Mountain-breaker, into the mouth of the buried giant, Wainamoinen mightily thrust his staff of smithied iron.

And Kalewa awoke from his slumber of ages,—awoke with groans of pain,—and he closed his jaws upon the staff; but his teeth could not crush the core of steel, could not shatter the staff of iron. And as Kalewa opened wider his mouth to devour the tormentor, lo! Wainamoinen leaped into the yawning throat and descended into the monstrous entrails. And Wainamoinen kindled a flame in the giant's belly,—built him a forge in his entrails.

Then Kalewa, in his great agony, called on that god who leans upon the axis of the world, and upon the blue goddesses of the waters, and upon the deities of the icy wildernesses, and upon the spirits of the forest, and even upon the great Jumala, at whose birth the brazen mountains trembled and lakes were changed into hills. But the gods came not to aid him.

Then Kalewa cursed his tormentor with a thousand magical curses, with curses of wind and storm and fire, with curses that change men's faces into stone, with curses that transport the accursed to the vast deserts of Laponia, where the hoof of the horse is never heard, where the children of the mare can find no pasturage. But the curses harmed not Wainamoinen; the curses only called forth the laughter of scorn from the lips of Wainamoinen.

And Wainamoinen cried out unto Kalewa: "Never shall I depart from hence, O thou mightiest singer of runes, until I have learned from thee the three magical words which I desire, the three words of enchantment that I have sought throughout the world in vain. Sing to me, O Kalewa, thy songs, thy most wondrous songs, thy marvellous songs of enchantment."

So the giant Kalewa, the possessor of sublimest wisdom, the singer of marvellous runes, opened his mouth and sang his songs for Wainamoinen, his most wondrous songs, his wizard songs.

Words succeeded to words, verses to verses, wizard runes to wizard runes. Ere Kalewa could sing all that he knew, could utter all that he had learned, the mountains would cease to be, the waters of the rivers would dry up, the great lakes be depopulated of their finny people, the sea have forgotten its power to make waves.

Unceasingly he sang for many days, unceasingly for many sleepless nights; he sang the songs of wizards, the songs of enchantment, the songs that create or destroy.

He sang the songs of wisdom, the runes sung by the gods before the beginning of the world, the verses by whose utterance nothingness became substance and darkness became light.

And as he sang the fair Sun paused in her course to hear him; the golden Moon stopped in her path to listen; the awful billows of the sea stood still; the icy rivers that devour the pines, that swallow up the firs, ceased to rage; the mighty cataracts hung motionless above their abysses; the waves of Juortana lifted high their heads to hear.

And Wainamoinen heard at last the three words, the three magical words, he sought for; and he ceased tormenting Kalewa, and departed from him. So Kalewa sank again into his eternal slumber, and the earth that loved him recovered him, and the forests rewove their network of knotted roots above his place of sleep.

Kalapana

HAWAII

"*Aloha*, old man! Where are you from, and why do you paddle to Puna?" The old man pulled his canoe up on the sand and stood panting. He was a queer figure, tall and bony, with long white hair tangled by the wind.

Tired from handling the canoe he could not speak at first. At last he said, "My name is Kalapana. I come from Kauai. All my life I have longed to see Pele, that great goddess of the volcano. I made a promise that, until I could see her, I would never cut my hair. There has been much to do, time has passed and now I am an old man. But the wish is still strong in my heart. I have kept my promise, and at last I come to Hawaii, the island of Pele."

The man of Puna looked at the old man's thin legs, then turned to glance at the mountain. "The trail is long," he said. "This day is nearly done. Come home with me, Kalapana, to rest and eat."

Very thankfully Kalapana followed his new friend. Rest and food were good! He slept next morning until the sun was high. When he awoke he went at once to the door. "I must go!" he said. "I can hardly wait now that I have reached Hawaii."

"Not today!" his friend answered. "Here the sun is bright, but clouds lie thick in the upland. You would find fog and rain. The rocks would be slippery and you might lose the trail."

Impatiently the old man waited. He walked about the village and watched people at their work. He was greeted kindly, though some laughed at his long tangled hair. "It is a promise," his friend explained. "Long ago Kalapana promised he would never cut his hair until he had looked upon Pele, goddess of the fire pit."

"What if someone cut it for him?" one boy whispered to another.

The other looked at him questioningly. "Do we dare?" he whispered back.

Three days Kalapana waited. On the fourth his friend called him early. "The time has come," he said. "Today the sun shines even on the mountaintop. Here is food, for the trail is long. Start now while the day is cool. Be strong for the journey and may you have success!" He guided Kalapana on his way, showed him the trail, and watched the old man till he became small in the distance.

For a time Kalapana climbed eagerly. Then, as the trail became steep and the sun hot, he went more slowly. He stopped in the shade of a small tree, ate a bit from his *ti*-leaf bundle and rested. Then he went on.

As he tramped steadily over old lava flows and across dry plains, he thought of Pele, the beautiful goddess whom he was soon to see. The trail led up and up. The rocks had been hot under his feet, but now they were cool. The sun no longer beat upon the old man and he was glad. Glancing up he saw a sheltering cloud. It was good to be out of the burning sun, and he sat down to rest and catch his breath. Then he went on.

Suddenly rain! It poured about him like a waterfall. The old man slipped and fell. He got to his feet but could not find the trail. He tried to go on, but the rain blinded him. It blew in his face and beat his body as if it meant to drive him back. At last, tired out, Kalapana gave up the struggle and started down. Now wind and rain were helping him. He found the trail and followed it.

The way was easy now and the rain had stopped. "I will

finish my journey," the old man thought, though his body ached with the struggle. But when he turned, he saw that rain was still falling higher up the mountain. A wall of storm seemed to bar his way. Kalapana went back to the village by the sea.

Tired and weak after his climb and drenching, the old man was glad to rest for several days. Then again, his friend said that Kilauea was clear of rain clouds. Again the old man started.

This time he got far up the mountain. The climb was not so steep now, and the trail led over old lava flows and around small craters. "I have almost reached her!" Kalapana thought. "Today my life's dream will come true. I shall see Pele!"

But again a storm struck him. Blinding rain drove him back. He tried to go on but could not. Tired out, at last he staggered down the trail.

"It is very strange," his friend said. "Here the sun has shone all day. It may be Pele does not want you to see her face. Come now, eat and rest."

Kalapana was too tired to eat. He threw himself upon the mats in the warm house, and sleep came quickly. It was sound sleep. The old man did not hear the evening noises as people made ready for the night. In the silence that followed, he did not hear the whispers of two boys or smell the odor of burning hair.

Toward morning he was wakened by hearing his name: "O Kalapana!" He opened his eyes and saw a woman standing by his mats. He could see her plainly—tall and more beautiful than any woman his eyes had ever looked upon. Her *paʻu* was dyed red, and she wore leis of red *lehua*. Her eyes were very bright, but they were kind. He knew that she was Pele and, in his joy, he could neither speak nor move.

"O Kalapana, I have come to you," the goddess said. "I did not want you to come to me in the fire pit. So I sent a storm to turn you back. But, O Kalapana, why have you cut your hair?"

He tried to say, "I have not cut it," but no words came. He raised his hand and felt his hair. He felt short ends and smelled the odor of burning. Someone had cut his hair—cut it with fire!

"I understand," Pele said, and her voice was kind. "It was not you who cut it, but some bad boys. Your punishment will not be great, but because your promise was not kept, you must not return to your own island. You must live and die in Puna."

Slowly the goddess disappeared. Kalapana lay quiet and content. He had seen Pele! It did not matter that his hair was gone, for she understood the reason. She had come to him and he had seen her loveliness!

In the morning he told his friend what had passed in the night. "If you are to stay in Puna, you must live with me," the friend said. "You can care for my garden while I fish. Stay as my companion."

So Kalapana stayed. The boys wondered at his happiness. "I have seen Pele!" he said. "My life's dream has come true." He had forgotten about his hair.

The old man went quietly about the village. He cared for his friend's garden and helped the neighbors, playing with a baby or gathering shellfish and seaweed.

His face was always full of joy. "I have seen Pele!" he said often, and he told those who would listen how the goddess had stood by his mats and spoken to him.

People came to love and respect the old man, and when he died they named their district for him—Kalapana.

The Great Jaguar

GUATEMALA/MAYA

Long ago there was an old man who had several head of cattle widely scattered on the pastures of *Huntah* but, since these regions were very mountainous at that time, the man always went to look for his herds accompanied by his hunting dogs.

One time when the man was walking through those mountains, his three dogs began to bark at the foot of a tree. He went to see what the dogs were after. Upon seeing that it was a fierce jaguar his dogs had treed, he decided to call them off the hunt. The man knew how dangerous it was to confront such a wild animal.

The old man was about to leave the area when a young campesino appeared and asked, "Señor, what are your dogs chasing?"

"My dogs have treed a jaguar. This is a very dangerous beast and it's better that we leave."

"Have no fear. I believe today we shall eat meat," said the campesino.

"Aha, if you believe you are sufficiently quick to defend yourself, then go take a look," the old man told him.

"All right, let's go hunting. Come along with me and don't worry," the young man said. He prepared a good rope for his use.

As they approached the jaguar, he prepared for his attack. In this moment the jaguar threw himself upon the old man instead of on the young worker. When the young man saw how furiously the jaguar attacked, he hid himself. Meanwhile the old man, with extraordinary skill with the machete, began to fight the beast. Fortunately the dogs also began to attack the jaguar, and this gave the old man the chance to deliver well aimed blows. The old man and the dogs continued fighting the beast until he managed to deliver a deadly blow to the head. With this the jaguar fell to the ground and the three dogs moved in. Soon the jaguar gave up and died.

"Wow! Is it already dead?" shouted the young man from his hiding place.

"Yes, come here and look," replied the old man, his blood still boiling from the fight.

The young man was afraid to come out from his hiding place because the old man was still swinging the machete furiously. After a long while the old man called the young man again. "Hey, come here and take a look. Don't be afraid."

"Don't hurt me, please, señor," shouted the young campesino.

"No. Come with me. My blood has cooled and my nerves have returned to normal," the old man said.

The young man approached, saying, "Señor, I hope that nothing has happened to you."

"To me—nothing. But I only want to tell you that if at some time you find this kind of animal, don't dare to confront it, because it is not easily defeated."

So said the old man, counseling the young man to avoid unnecessary problems and dangers. If they escaped that adventure with their lives, it was thanks to the fierceness of the hunting dogs, and above all to the bravery of this old campesino.

The Hunted Hare

ENGLAND

Once upon a time there was an old woman who lived by herself on the edge of the great wild moor. Many tales the folk thereabouts told of fiends, and spirits, and all manner of fearful things that roamed the moor at night. You may be sure they took care never to be abroad on that bleak stretch of lonely land once darkness had fallen.

Now it happened the old woman had to cross the moor once a week to reach the market town to sell her butter and eggs. She usually rose early, just before dawn, to set out. One night, knowing the next day to be market day, she went to bed quite early. When she awoke, she began to get ready for her journey. It was still dark, of course, and, having no clock, she did not know it was still before midnight. She dressed, ate, saddled her horse, and attached to it the large wicker panniers containing the butter and eggs. Wrapping a worn old cloak about her, she and the horse sleepily set off across the moor.

She had not gone very far before she heard the sounds of a pack of hounds baying under the stars and saw, racing toward her, a white hare. When it reached her, the hare leaped up on a large rock close by the path as if to say, "Come, catch me."

The old woman chuckled. She liked the idea of outwitting the hounds, so she reached out her hand, picked up the crouching hare, and popped it into one of her wicker panniers. She dropped the lid and rode on.

The baying of the hounds came nearer, and suddenly she saw a headless horse galloping toward her, surrounded by a pack of monstrous hounds. On the horse sat a dark figure with horns sprouting out of his head. The eyes of the hounds shone fiery red, while their tails glowed with a blue flame.

It was a terrifying sight to behold. Her horse stood trembling and shaking, but the woman sat up boldly to confront the horned demon. She had the hare in her basket and didn't intend to give it up. But it seemed that these monstrous creatures were not very clever or knowing, for the rider asked the old woman, very civilly, had she seen a white hare run past and did she know in which direction it had gone.

"No indeed," she said firmly. "I saw no hare run past me." Which of course was true.

The rider spurred his headless horse, called his hounds to follow, and galloped across the moors. When they were out of sight, the woman patted and calmed her shivering horse.

Suddenly, to her surprise, the lid of the pannier moved and then opened. It was no frightened hare who came forth, but a woman all in white.

The ghostly lady spoke in a clear voice. "Dame," she said, "I admire your courage. You have saved me from a terrible enchantment and now the spell is broken. I am no human woman—it was my fate to be condemned for centuries to the form of a hare and to be pursued on the moor at night by evil demons until I could get behind their tails while they passed on in search of me. Through your courage the enchantment is broken, and I can now return to my own kind. We will never forget you. I promise that all your hens shall lay two eggs instead of one, your cows shall give plenty of milk year round, your garden crops shall thrive and yield a fine harvest. But beware the devil fiend and his evil spirits, for he will try to do you harm once he realizes you were clever enough to outwit him. May good fortune attend you."

The mysterious lady vanished and was never seen again, but all she promised came true. The woman had the best possible luck at market that morning and continued to have good fortune with all her crops and livestock. The devil never did succeed in getting revenge—though he had many a try— and the kindly protection of the ghostly lady stayed with the woman the rest of her life.

The Apparition of Arran

SCOTLAND

About a century ago there lived in Arran an old woman named Marie Nic Junraidh, or Mary Henderson, who was exceedingly diminutive, but very courageous and intelligent. She was returning home late, one dark night, and had to cross a bridge which had the reputation of being haunted by something awful, and at which bold strong men had been terrified. But although it was night-time and dark, yet the bold little woman took courage to cross the bridge; and when she came to it, she saw something of an awful appearance standing before her. She would not turn back; so she spake to it, and it spake to her again, and then assumed a human shape, which she readily recognized, and said, "*An tu Fionla?*" ["Art thou Finlay?"] The appearance answered that he was Finlay. She said that she had known him when he was alive, but that he had died some years before. He said it was quite true; and that he was the same Finlay.

"Then what is the reason," she said, "that you appear before a frail little woman, and seek thus to alarm me? Why did you not appear before strong men, if you had anything upon your mind that you wished to tell?"

"I did appear several times to strong men," answered the spirit; "but they were always frightened, and ran away without speaking to me. You have done well to stay and speak to me, and I can now ease my mind. When I was in the flesh I stole some plough-irons; and I can get no rest until they are restored to their rightful owner. So you will go tomorrow, without fail, to yonder place, and there you will find the plough-irons; and if you will take them and lay them by the wayside, I shall get my rest, and I will not trouble you or any other person after this."

The little woman then took courage and proposed many questions to the apparition, all of which he readily answered. He told her how long she would live, also her husband and other members of her family. He also told her the state of her departed friends and neighbours; and told her to warn a certain neighbour to give up his evil doings, for that he was in great danger. She promised that she would attend to all his demands; and he then vanished and allowed her to cross the bridge and get safely to her own home. The next morning she went to the spot and found the plough-irons, which she took and left by the wayside, where their previous owner found them; but it was observed that he did not live long after picking them up. She gave the warning to the neighbour, and he received it and repented him of his sins; and both she and her husband died at the time that had been foretold. After her interview with the spirit, the bridge was not haunted by night, nor was anyone troubled by the apparition.

The Valiant Fish Trapper

HUNGARY

There's a village by the name of Luka. There's a lake there, named Lake Varjános after a certain János Var. In the days of Turkish rule, the villagers of Luka woke one day to find some one hundred and fifty Turks holding a nearby hill. Wailing and lamenting, the people of the village gathered on the opposite hill, where the church stood.

"What's to become of us! The Turks will kill us all. We'll surely perish if we fall into their hands."

There was an old man named János Var. He made his living by trapping fish in weirs set up in the lake. Also, he used to go to a nearby wood and collect the eggs from the nests of the birds, and sometimes he went to help the fishermen.

When he heard the wailing and lamenting of his fellow villagers, he stepped up to the magistrate and asked him, "What's wrong with the people, sir? Why are they lamenting?"

"Sure, there's reason enough. Just look at that hill over there. The Turks will be here in no time to cut off our heads."

Old János Var said, "No need to worry about that, sir. Just let me deal with the Turks."

The others waited to see how he would be going about it. They saw him row over to the opposite side of the lake. When he got ashore he made for the hill and walked straight up to the Turks. From his gestures they could guess that he was trying to persuade them to get into his punt. But it was a very small boat, only able to hold one person, besides himself. The Turks thought that he was offering to take them over to the village, and so one Turk got into the boat. When János got to that part of the lake where the water turns into a reed-filled swamp, old János just tilted the boat. The Turk fell into the water, and when he bobbed up again old János hit him on the head with the punt pole and pushed him down, keeping him under water with the pole until he saw the last bubbles coming up. When he had finished with one Turk, he went back for the next one. Since the Turks could not see what was happening in the reed-filled swamp, they had no idea of what had happened to their comrades. They thought that the old man had taken their companions to the village where they would be waiting for the rest to come. But old János did away with the whole lot of them, drowning one after the other in the lake.

When he had finished off the hundred and fifty to the last man, János went back to the magistrate and said, "Well, sir, I've saved the village from the Turks. There was no need to make such a fuss about them."

Before then uncle János had been a poor cotter, but after this piece of gallantry he was raised to noble rank and was given a large estate.

Grandmother Spider Steals the Fire

The Choctaw People say that when the People first came up out of the ground, People were encased in cocoons, their eyes closed, their limbs folded tightly to their bodies. And this was true of all People: the Bird People, the Animal People, the Insect People, and the Human People. The Great Spirit took pity on them, and sent down someone to unfold their limbs, dry them off, and open their eyes. But the opened eyes saw nothing, because the world was dark: no sun, no moon, not even any stars. All the People moved around by touch, and if they found something that didn't eat them first, they ate it raw, for they had no fire to cook it.

All the People met in a great powwow, with the Animal and Bird People taking the lead, and the Human People hanging back. The Animal and Bird People decided that life was not good, but cold and miserable. A solution must be found! Someone spoke from the dark, "I have heard that the people in the East have fire." This caused a stir of wonder, "What could fire be?" There was a general discussion, and it was decided that if, as rumor had it, fire was warm and gave light, they should have it too. Another voice said, "But the people of the East are too greedy to share with us." So it was decided that the Bird and Animal People should *steal* what they needed: the fire!

But, who should have the honor? Grandmother Spider

volunteered: "I can do it! Let me try!" But at the same time, Opossum began to speak. "I, Opossum, am a great chief of the animals. I will go to the East, and since I am a great hunter, I will take the fire and hide it in the bushy hair on my tail." It was well known that Opossum had the furriest tail of all the animals, so he was selected.

When Opossum came to the East, he soon found the beautiful red fire, jealously guarded by the people of the East. But Opossum got closer and closer until he picked up a small piece of burning wood, and stuck it in the hair of his tail, which promptly began to smoke, then flame. The people of the East said, "Look, that Opossum has stolen our fire!" They took it and put it back where it came from and drove Opossum away. Poor Opossum! Every bit of hair had burned from his tail, and to this day, opossums have no hair at all on their tails.

Once again, the powwow had to find a volunteer chief. Grandmother Spider again said, "Let me go! I can do it!" But this time, a bird was elected—Buzzard. Buzzard was very proud. "I can succeed where Opossum has failed. I will fly to the East on my great wings, then hide the stolen fire in the beautiful long feathers on my head." The birds and animals still did not understand the nature of fire. So Buzzard flew to the East on his powerful wings, swooped past those defending the fire, picked up a small piece of burning ember, and hid it in his head feathers. Buzzard's head began to smoke and flame even faster! The people of the East said, "Look! Buzzard has stolen the fire!" And they took it and put it back where it came from.

Poor Buzzard! His head was now bare of feathers, red

and blistered looking. And to this day, buzzards have naked heads that are bright red and blistered.

The powwow now sent Crow to look the situation over, for Crow was very clever. Crow at that time was pure white, and had the sweetest singing voice of all the birds. But he took so long standing over the fire, trying to find the perfect piece to steal, that his white feathers were smoked black. And he breathed so much smoke that when he tried to sing, out came a harsh "Caw! Caw!"

The Council said, "Opossum has failed. Buzzard and Crow have failed. Who shall we send?"

Tiny Grandmother Spider shouted with all her might, "LET ME TRY IT, PLEASE!" Though the council members thought Grandmother Spider had little chance of success, it was agreed that she should have her turn. Grandmother Spider looked then like she looks now—she had a small torso suspended by two sets of legs that turned up toward her head and two sets of legs that turned the other way. She walked on all of her wonderful legs toward a stream where she had found clay. With those legs, she made a tiny clay container and a lid that fit perfectly with a tiny notch for air in the corner of the lid. Then she put the container on her back, spun a web all the way to the East, and walked on tip-toe until she came to the fire. She was so small, the people from the East took no notice. She took a tiny piece of fire, put it in the container, and covered it with the lid. Then she walked back on tip-toe along the web until she came to the People. Since they couldn't see any fire, they said, "Grandmother Spider has failed."

"Oh, no," she said, "I have the fire!" She lifted the pot

from her back, and the lid from the pot, and the fire flamed up into its friend, the air. All the Bird and Animal People began to decide who would get this wonderful warmth. Bear said, "I'll take it!" but then he burned his paws on it and decided fire was not for animals, for look what happened to Opossum!

The birds wanted no part of it, as Buzzard and Crow were still nursing their wounds. The insects thought it was pretty, but they, too, stayed far away from the fire.

Then a small voice said, "We will take it, if Grandmother Spider will help." The timid humans, whom none of the animals or birds thought much of, were volunteering!

So Grandmother Spider taught the Human People how to feed the fire sticks and wood to keep it from dying, how to keep the fire safe in a circle of stone so it couldn't escape and hurt them or their homes. While she was at it, she taught the humans about pottery made of clay and fire, and about weaving and spinning, at which Grandmother Spider was an expert.

The Choctaw remember. They made a beautiful design to decorate their homes: a picture of Grandmother spider, two sets of legs up, two down, with a fire symbol on her back. This is so their children never forget to honor Grandmother Spider—Firebringer!

The Monster of Loch Garten

SCOTLAND

Amid the Abernethy Forest in Strath Spey lies lovely Loch Garten darkened by pine woods and birch trees.

Tradition has it that a large carnivorous water-monster—a cross between a huge bull and a large stallion—used to haunt the neighbourhood where a burn (about ¼ mile long) flows out of Loch Garten into Loch Mallachie, through thick woods. This ugly creature, believed to prey on children and lambs, was described as having a jet-black mane, big head, broad back and glistening eyes. It wandered forth at night-time and its roars were to be heard echoing amongst the hills.

According to a local story, an old crofter from Nethy Bridge decided to capture the beast, and one afternoon hitched the end of a long rope round a large boulder weighing several tons, on the shore of Loch Garten, at the other end of which he affixed a gaff-hook which he baited with a lamb. After he had coiled the rest of the line into a dinghy, he pushed off from the bank and paid out the rope yard by yard as he rowed towards the centre of the loch. When he had come to the end of the cordage, he heaved the baited hook (which he had appropriately weighted) overboard and rowed back to land as the afternoon was drawing to a close.

All through that night, there was a tremendous storm. Over and above the roar of the thunder and the noise of the tempest, came the fiendish snarls of the infuriated monster.

In the morning, after the storm had subsided, when the old man returned to the loch-side, not a trace of the huge rock could he discover. All that could be seen was a long deep-rooted rut along the trend of the sand leading down to the water's edge where the boulder had been dragged into the inky depths by the monster, which has not been seen or heard of since.

The Woman in the Moon

HAWAII

Long ago there lived a woman named Hina who had lived for many years. Day after day she made tapa cloth out of the bark of a tree by beating it with a mallet. Then she used the cloth to make clothing for her family. Her son and daughter had finally grown up and left home, leaving her with a husband who had become more embittered and demanding as he grew older. He offered her no help or companionship.

Each night when her cloth making was finished and the sun went down, she would fetch water with a gourd, fix the dinner, and pray for rest from her endless tasks. She would think about how she might escape from her weary existence and find peace. One day she was pounding out the tapa cloth and cried aloud, "If only I could go away and find some rest!"

The rainbow heard Hina's cry and set a rainbow in front

of her. Hina decided she would follow the rainbow up to heaven and then to the sun, where she would be forever at rest. She began her long journey up the rainbow, but when she passed through the clouds the sun's rays began to burn her. She pushed herself to continue, but the rays became too hot. The sun began to singe her hair and skin, and she felt her strength ebbing away. She let her body slide back down the rainbow, grieving at her failure.

When she had returned to earth, darkness had descended. As she came to her house she saw that her husband had fetched the water. He was grumbling about this chore, and when he saw her he reprimanded her for being gone from the house. His words strengthened her resolve to find quiet and rest. She noticed that the sun was gone, and as she stared at the quiet coolness of the moon she realized it would be a far better place to rest than the sun.

Before she left again, she entered the house and gathered up all the possessions that were dear to her and placed them in an empty gourd. As she left the house she saw that the rainbow had not deserted her, but had arched to the moon. Her husband followed her out and when he saw her with her belongings he knew she was not returning soon.

"Where are you going, my wife?" he asked brusquely.

"I am going to the moon where I can rest quietly," she answered.

She began to climb the rainbow, but her husband cried out in anger, grabbed her foot, and pulled her down. Hina felt the bones in her foot break as they fell together to earth, but she pulled herself up and started up the rainbow once again. Her husband was too stunned at her determination to try to stop her again.

Hina's lameness and the pain slowed her, but her heart filled with joy as she continued to climb up the rainbow. She climbed until she came to the stars and prayed they would guide her to the moon. The stars heard her prayer and led her onward.

Finally she came to the moon. It guided her to a place where she could keep her belongings and rest. Hina was over-joyed. She knew she would never leave this place of peace and quiet.

These days the people of Hawaii look up at the moon and see Hina there with her gourd of precious possessions at her side. Her foot is still lame, but her serenity and benevo-lence soothe all who take the time to look.

The Hedley Kow

ENGLAND

There was once an old woman, who earned a poor living by going errands and such like, for the farmers' wives round about the village where she lived. It wasn't much she earned by it; but with a plate of meat at one house, and a cup of tea at another, she made shift to get on somehow, and always looked as cheerful as if she hadn't a want in the world.

Well, one summer evening as she was trotting away home-wards she came upon a big black pot lying at the side of the road.

"Now *that*," said she, stopping to look at it, "would be just the very thing for me if I had anything to put into it! But who can have left it here?" and she looked round about, as if the person it belonged to must be not far off. But she could see no one.

"Maybe it'll have a hole in it," she said thoughtfully: "Ay, that'll be how they've left it lying, hinny. But then it'd do fine to put a flower in for the window; I'm thinking I'll just take it home, anyways." And she bent her stiff old back, and lifted the lid to look inside.

"Mercy me!" she cried, and jumped back to the other side of the road; "*if it isn't brim full o' gold* PIECES!!"

For a while she could do nothing but walk round and round her treasure, admiring the yellow gold and wondering at her good luck, and saying to herself about every two min-utes, "Well, I *do* be feeling rich and grand!" But presently she began to think how she could best take it home with her; and she couldn't see any other way than by fastening one end of her shawl to it, and so dragging it after her along the road.

"It'll certainly be soon dark," she said to herself, "and folk'll not see what I'm bringing home with me, and so I'll have all the night to myself to think what I'll do with it. I could buy a grand house and all, and live like the Queen her-self, and not do a stroke of work all day, but just sit by the fire with a cup of tea; or maybe I'll give it to the priest to keep for me, and get a piece as I'm wanting; or maybe I'll just bury it in a hole at the garden-foot, and put a bit on the chimney, between the chiney teapot and the spoons—for ornament, like. Ah! I feel so grand, I don't know myself rightly!"

And by this time, being already rather tired with dragging such a heavy weight after her, she stopped to rest for a minute, turning to make sure that her treasure was safe.

But when she looked at it, it wasn't a pot of gold at all, but a great lump of shining silver!

She stared at it, and rubbed her eyes and stared at it again; but she couldn't make it look like anything but a great lump of silver. "I'd have sworn it was a pot of gold," she said at last, "but I reckon I must have been dreaming. Ay, now, that's a change for the better; it'll be far less trouble to look after, and none so easy stolen; yon gold pieces would have been a sight of bother to keep 'em safe—Ay, I'm well quit of them; and with my bonny lump I'm as rich as rich—!"

And she set off homewards again, cheerfully planning all the grand things she was going to do with her money. It wasn't very long, however, before she got tired again and stopped once more to rest for a minute or two.

Again she turned to look at her treasure, and as soon as she set eyes on it she cried out in astonishment. "Oh my!" said she; "now it's a lump o' iron! Well, that beats all; and it's just real convenient! I can sell it as *easy* as *easy*, and get a lot o' penny pieces for it. Ay, hinny, an' it's much handier than a lot o' yer gold and silver as'd have kept me from sleeping o' nights thinking the neighbours were robbing me—an' it's a real good thing to have by you in a house, ye niver can tell what ye mightn't use it for, an' it'll sell—ay, for a real lot. Rich? I'll be just *rolling!*"

And on she trotted again chuckling to herself on her good luck, till presently she glanced over her shoulder, "just to make sure it was there still," as she said to herself.

"Eh my!" she cried as soon as saw it; "if it hasn't gone and turned itself into a great stone this time! Now, how could it have known that I was just *terrible* wanting something to hold my door open with? Ay, if that isn't a good change! Hinny, it's a fine thing to have such good luck."

And, all in a hurry to see how the stone would look in its corner by her door, she trotted off down the hill, and stopped at the foot, beside her own little gate.

When she had unlatched it, she turned to unfasten her shawl from the stone, which this time seemed to lie unchanged and peaceably on the path beside her. There was still plenty of light, and she could see the stone quite plainly as she bent her stiff back over it, to untie the shawl end; when, all of a sudden, it seemed to give a jump and a squeal, and grew in a moment as big as a great horse; then it threw down four lanky legs, and shook out two long ears, flourished a tail, and went off kicking its feet into the air, and laughing like a naughty mocking boy.

The old woman stared after it, till it was fairly out of sight.

"WELL!" she said at last, "I *do* be the luckiest body hereabouts! Fancy me seeing the Hedley Kow all to myself, and making so free with it, too! I can tell you, I *do* feel that GRAND—"

And she went into her cottage and sat down by the fire to think over her good luck.

The Search for Luck

GREECE

To go on and on with the story: there was an old woman and she had a hen. Like her the hen was well on in years and a good worker: every day she laid an egg. The old woman had a neighbour, an old man, a plague-stricken old fellow, and whenever the old woman went off anywhere he used to steal the egg. The poor old woman kept a lookout to catch the thief, but she could never succeed, nor did she want to make accusations against anyone, so she had the idea of going to ask the Undying Sun.

As she was on the way she met three sisters: all three of them were old maids. When they saw her, they ran after her to find out where she was going. She told them what her trouble had been. "And now," said she, "I am on my way to ask the Undying Sun and find out what son of a bitch this can be who steals my eggs and does such cruelty to a poor tired old woman." When the girls heard this they threw themselves upon her shoulders:

"O Auntie, I beg you, ask him about us; what is the matter with us that we can't get married." "Very well," said the old woman. "I will ask him, and perhaps he may attend to what I say."

So she went on and on and she met an old woman shivering with cold. When the old woman saw her and heard where she was going, she began to entreat her: "I beg you, old woman, to question him about me, too; what is the matter with me that I can never be warm although I wear three fur coats, all one on top of the other." "Very well," said the old woman, "I will ask him, but how can I help you?"

So she went on and on and she came to a river; it ran turbid and dark as blood. From a long way off she heard its rushing sound and her knees shook with fear. When the river saw her he, too, asked her in a savage and angry voice where she was going. She said to him what she had to say. The river said to her: "If this is so, ask him about me, too: what plague is this upon me that I can never flow at ease." "Very well, my dear river; very well," said the old woman in such terror that she hardly knew how to go on.

So she went on and on, and came to a monstrous great rock; it had for very many years been hanging suspended and could neither fall nor not fall. The rock begged the old woman to ask what was oppressing it so that it could not fall and be at rest and passers-by be free from fear. "Very well," said the old woman, "I will ask him; it is not much to ask and I will take it upon me."

Talking in this way the old woman found it was very late and so she lifted up her feet and how she did run! When she came up to the crest of the mountain, there she saw the Undying Sun combing his beard with his golden comb. As soon as he saw her he bade her welcome and gave her a stool and then asked her why she had come. The old woman told him what she had suffered about the eggs laid by her hen: "And I throw myself at your feet," said she: "tell me who the thief is. I wish I knew, for then I should not be cursing him so madly and laying a burden on my soul. Also, please see here: I have brought you a kerchief full of pears from my garden and a basket full of baked rolls." Then the Undying Sun said to her: "The man who steals your eggs is that neighbour of yours. Yet see that you say nothing to him; leave him to God and the man will come by his deserts."

"As I was on my way," said the old woman to the Undying Sun, "I came upon three girls, unmarried, and how they did entreat me! 'Ask about us; what is the matter with us that we get no husbands.' " "I know who you mean. They are not girls anyone will marry. They are like to be idle; they have no mother to guide them nor father either, and so it happens that every day they start and sweep the house out without sprinkling water and then use the broom and fill my eyes with dust and how sick I am of them! I can't bear them. Tell them that from henceforth they must rise before dawn and sprinkle the house and then sweep, and very soon they will get husbands. You need have no more thought about them as you go your way."

"Then an old woman made a request of me: 'Ask him on my behalf what is the matter with me that I cannot keep warm although I wear three fur coats one on top of the other.' " "You must tell her to give away two in charity for the sake of her soul and then she will keep warm."

"Also I saw a river turbid and dark as blood; its flow entangled with eddies. The river requested me: 'Ask him about me; what can I do to flow at ease?' " "The river must drown a man and so it will be at ease. When you get there, first cross over the stream and then say what I have said to you; otherwise the river will take you as its prey."

"Also I saw a rock: years and years have passed and all the

time it has hung like this suspended and cannot fall." "This rock too must bring a man to death and thus it will be at ease. When you go there pass by the rock, and not till then, say what I have said to you."

The old woman arose and kissed his hand and said Farewell and went down from the mountain. On her way she came to the rock, and the rock was waiting for her coming as it were with five eyes. She made haste and passed beyond and then she said what she had been told to say to the rock. When the rock heard how he must fall and that to the death of a man, he grew angry; what to do he knew not. "Ah," said he to the old woman: "If you had told me that before, then I would have made you my prey." "May all my troubles be yours," said the old woman and she—pray excuse me— slapped her behind.

On her way she came close to the river and from the roar it was making she saw how troubled it was and that it was just waiting for her to hear what the Undying Sun had said to her. She made haste and crossed over the stream, and then she said what he had told her. When the river heard this, it was enraged, and such was its evil mood that the water was more turbid than ever. "Ah," said the river, "why did I not know this? Then I would have had your life, you who are an old woman whom nobody wants." The old woman was so much frightened that she never turned round to look at the river.

Before she had gone much farther she could see the reek coming up from the roofs of the village and the savour of cooking came across to her. She made no delay but went to the old woman, she who could never keep warm, and said to her what she had been told to say. The table was set all fresh and she sat down and ate with them: they had fine lenten fare and you would have eaten and licked your fingers, so good it was.

Then she went to find the old maids. From the time the old woman had left them their minds had been on her; they were neither lighting the fire in their house nor putting it out: all the time they had their eyes on the road to see the old woman when she came by. As soon as the old woman saw them, she went and sat down and explained to them that they must do what the Undying Sun had told her to tell them. After this they rose up always when it was still night and sprinkled the floor and swept it, and then suitors began to come again, some from one place and some from another; all to ask them in marriage. So they got husbands and lived and were happy.

As for the old woman who could never keep warm, she gave away two of her fur coats for the good of her soul and at once found herself warm. The river and the rock each took a man's life and so they were at rest.

When the old woman came back home she found the old man at the very gate of death. When she had gone off to find the Undying Sun he was so much frightened that a terrible thing happened to him: the hen's feathers grew out of his face. No long time passed before he went off to that big village whence no man ever returns. After that the eggs were never missing and the old woman ate them until she died, and when she died the hen died, too.

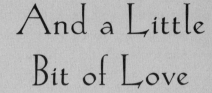

And a Little Bit of Love

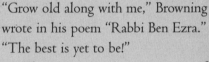

"Grow old along with me," Browning wrote in his poem "Rabbi Ben Ezra." "The best is yet to be!"

That sentiment sometimes sets off snickers.

The elderly are too often seen as asexual beings, yet polls prove otherwise. While the frequency of lovemaking may have slowed, the older folks still own up to romantic entanglements and sexual desires.

And the folklore knows it, too.

There are folk stories that deal with the love life of older people. Sometimes the stories are little more than jokes, tales that are characterized by folklorist Stith Thompson as "humorous or scurrilous anecdotes of married life so popular in the fabliaux." Sometimes the stories are rhapsodic about the length of time two people have been in love. "Baucis and Philemon" is the classic example. And some—like the Syrian story "The Cure"—are about the fact that sex can still be of interest to a ninety-year-old.

Baucis and Philemon

GREECE

On a certain hill in Phyrgia stands a linden tree and an oak, enclosed by a low wall. Not far from the spot is a marsh, formerly good habitable land, but now indented with pools, the resort of fen-birds and cormorants. Once on a time Jupiter, in human shape, visited this country, and with him his son Mercury (he of the caduceus), without his wings. They presented themselves, as weary travellers, at many a door, seeking rest and shelter, but found all closed, for it was late, and the inhospitable inhabitants would not rouse themselves to open for their reception. At last a humble mansion received them, a small thatched cottage, where Baucis, a pious old dame, and her husband Philemon, united when young, had grown old together. Not ashamed of their poverty, they made it endurable by moderate desires and kind dispositions. One need not look there for master or for servant; they two were the whole household, master and servant alike. When the two heavenly guests crossed the humble threshold, and bowed their heads to pass under the low door, the old man placed a seat, on which Baucis, bustling and attentive, spread a cloth, and begged them to sit down. Then she raked out the coals from the ashes, and kindled up a fire, fed it with leaves and dry bark, and with her scanty breath blew it into a flame. She brought out of a corner split sticks and dry branches, broke them up, and placed them under the small kettle. Her husband collected some pot-herbs in the garden, and she shred them from the stalks, and prepared them for the pot. He reached down with a forked stick a flitch of bacon hanging in the chimney, cut a small piece, and put it in the pot to boil with the herbs, setting away the rest for another time. A beechen bowl was filled with warm water, that their guests might wash. While all was doing, they beguiled the time with conversation.

On the bench designed for the guests was laid a cushion stuffed with sea-weed; and a cloth, only produced on great occasions, but ancient and coarse enough, was spread over that. The old lady, with her apron on, with trembling hand set the table. One leg was shorter than the rest, but a piece of slate put under restored the level. When fixed, she rubbed the table down with some sweet-smelling herbs. Upon it she set some of chaste Minerva's olives, some cornel berries preserved in vinegar, and added radishes and cheese, with eggs lightly cooked in the ashes. All were served in earthen dishes, and an earthenware pitcher, with wooden cups, stood beside them. When all was ready, the stew, smoking hot, was set on the table. Some wine, not of the oldest, was added; and for dessert, apples and wild honey; and over and above all, friendly faces, and simple but hearty welcome.

Now while the repast proceeded, the old folks were astonished to see that the wine, as fast as it was poured out, renewed itself in the pitcher, of its own accord. Struck with terror, Baucis and Philemon recognized their heavenly guests, fell on their knees, and with clasped hands implored forgiveness for their poor entertainment. There was an old goose, which they kept as the guardian of their humble cottage, and they bethought them to make this a sacrifice in honour of their guests. But the goose, too nimble, with the aid of feet and wings, for the old folks, eluded their pursuit, and at last took shelter between the gods themselves. They forbade it to be slain; and spoke in these words: "We are gods. This inhospitable village shall pay the penalty of its impiety; you alone shall go free from the chastisement. Quit your house, and come with us to the top of yonder hill." They hastened to obey, and, staff in hand, laboured up the steep ascent. They had reached to within an arrow's flight of the top, when, turning their eyes below, they beheld all the country sunk in a lake, only their own house left standing. While they gazed with wonder at the sight, and lamented the fate of their neighbours, that old house of theirs was changed into a temple. Columns took the place of the corner posts, the thatch grew yellow and appeared a gilded roof, the floors became marble, the doors were enriched with carving and ornaments of gold. Then spoke Jupiter in benignant accents: "Excellent old man, and woman worthy of such a husband, speak, tell us your wishes; what favour have you to ask of us?" Philemon took counsel with Baucis a few moments; then declared to the gods their united wish. "We ask to be priests and guardians of this your temple; and since here we have passed our lives in love and concord, we wish that one and the same hour may take us both from life, that I may not live to see her grave, nor be laid in my own by her." Their prayer was granted. They were the keepers of the temple as long as they lived. When grown very old, as they stood one day before the steps of the sacred edifice, and were telling the story of the place, Baucis saw Philemon begin to put forth leaves, and old

Philemon saw Baucis changing in like manner. And now a leafy crown had grown over their heads, while exchanging parting words, as long as they could speak. "Farewell, dear spouse," they said, together, and at the same moment the bark closed over their mouths. The Tyanean shepherd still shows the two trees, standing side by side, made out of the two good old people.

How Much You Remind Me of My Husband!

EL SALVADOR

Once, there lived an old Indian and his wife in Huizúcar, in El Salvador. The old Indian worked and hunted as best he could, and his old wife worked as best she could. And so they lived through the years until one day the old Indian died.

His wife was quite sad. She was lonely now, like a person lost in a great forest. She worked a little, but most of the time she just sat on a wooden bench in front of her hut, in the shade of a large tree that grew there. She sat thinking of the days when her husband was living and they were happy together.

One day, as she was sitting on the bench shaded by the tree, she was saying, "How much I miss you, husband! How much I miss you! How I wish you were sitting by my side!"

She wished very, very hard, but it was no use. She still was sitting there all alone on the bench.

She looked up into the sky and saw a big buzzard flying around, moving in great circles. The buzzard looked down on the hut, the bench, and the woman. Then he looked at the tree beside her and decided this tree would be a fine place for him to rest. Slowly he flew lower and lower, and when he had selected the branch of the tree he liked best, he settled on it and made himself comfortable. The old Indian woman watched him flying around and around and finally alighting on the branch. She sat there looking at the buzzard, and the buzzard looked at her. They looked at each other for a long time.

Then the old woman said, "Oh, Tío Buzzard! How much you remind me of my dear dead husband! May his soul rest in peace! How much he looked like you! You are dressed just the same as he used to dress—his clothes were always black, just like your black feathers. He really looked like a buzzard. Oh, Tío Buzzard! How much you remind me of my dear husband!"

She paused, and then continued talking to the buzzard. "He wore a little white cap on his head just like yours. How you remind me of him! He always sat just as you sit, with his legs under him, hunched up. His head was always sunk deep between his shoulders, just like yours. How much you remind me of my dear dead husband! May he rest in peace."

She kept on talking and talking. The buzzard gazed at her solemnly. Suddenly he moved around in the branches, ruffling his feathers. As he did so, he broke off a thick branch. Buzzards are heavy birds, and his weight was too much for the branch to hold. It fell down on the old Indian woman, hitting her hard on the nose and cheek.

"Oh!" she cried. "That's just the way my husband used to hit me with a stick in the face! How much you remind me of him!"

Then the buzzard rose from the tree and slowly flew high up into the sky.

As he flew away, the old Indian woman gazed after him and said, "And there you are, flying away to Heaven, just as my husband did. How much alike you and my husband are!"

A Clever Old Bride

KOREA

In olden times early marriage was the rule, and very often the bride was considerably older than the bridegroom.

Once a rather elderly bride was married to a child-bridegroom. She tried to treat him as her husband, but he gave her no end of trouble by his childishness. She was ladling rice out of the pot one day when her husband came and asked her to give him the burnt rice at the bottom. She felt ashamed that her husband should be so childish, and so she snapped at him, "A gentleman mustn't ask for such things in the kitchen." Thereupon the boy burst into tears. She was greatly embarrassed by this, so she picked him up and put him on her back and started to soothe him like a baby. Before long he stopped crying.

Just then her husband's father came along. So she went to the door and told the boy to climb up the thatched roof where the gourds were growing. Then she said loudly, "Pick me a good ripe one, please." She did this to show her father-in-law that she had not been carrying her husband like a baby, for if it had been known she would never have been able to hold up her head again.

My Jon's Soul

ICELAND

There were once an old cottager and his wife who lived together. The old man was rather quarrelsome and disagreeable, and, what's more, he was lazy and useless about the house; his old woman was not at all pleased about it, and she would often grumble at him and say the only thing he was any good at was squandering what she had scraped together—for she herself was constantly at work and tried by hook or by crook to earn what they needed, and was always good at getting her own way with anybody she had to deal with. But even if they did not agree about some things, the old woman loved her husband dearly and never let him go short.

Now things went on the same way for a long time, but

one day the old man fell sick, and it was obvious that he was in a bad way. The old woman was sitting up with him, and when he grew weaker, it occurred to her that he could hardly be very well prepared for death, and that this meant there was some doubt as to whether he would be allowed to enter Heaven. So she thinks to herself that the best plan will be for her to try and put her husband's soul on the right road herself. Then she took a small bag and held it over her husband's nose and mouth, so that when the breath of life leaves him it passes into this bag, and she ties it up at once.

Then off she goes towards Heaven, carrying the bag in her apron, comes to the borders of the Kingdom of Heaven, and knocks on the door.

Out comes Saint Peter, and asks what her business may be.

"A very good morning to you, sir," says the old woman. "I've come here with the soul of that Jon of mine—you'll have heard tell of him, most likely—and now I'm wanting to ask you to let him in."

"Yes, yes, yes," says Peter, "but unfortunately I can't. I have indeed heard tell of that Jon of yours, but I never heard good of him yet."

Then the old woman said: "Well, really, Saint Peter, I'd never have believed it, that you could be so hard-hearted! You must be forgetting what happened to you in the old days, when you denied your Master."

At that, Peter went back in and shut the door, and the old woman remained outside, sighing bitterly. But when a little time has passed, she knocks on the door again, and out comes Saint Paul. She greets him and asks him his name, and he tells her who he is. Then she pleads with him for the soul of her Jon—but he said he didn't want to hear another word from her about that, and said that her Jon deserved no mercy.

Then the old woman got angry, and said: "It's all very well for you, Paul! I suppose you deserved mercy in the old days, when you were persecuting God and men! I reckon I'd better stop asking any favours from you."

So now Paul shuts the door as fast as he can. But when the old woman knocks for the third time, out comes the Blessed Virgin Mary.

"Hail, most blessed Lady," says the old woman. "I do hope you'll allow that Jon of mine in, even though that Peter and Paul won't allow it."

"It's a great pity, my dear," says Mary, "but I daren't, because he really was such a brute, that Jon of yours."

"Well, I can't blame you for that," says the old woman. "But all the same, I did think you would know that other people can have their little weaknesses as well as you—or have you forgotten by now that you once had a baby, and no father for it?"

Mary would hear no more, but shut the door as fast as she could.

For the fourth time, the old woman knocks on the door. Then out comes Christ himself, and asks what she's doing there.

Then she spoke very humbly: "I wanted to beg you, my dear Saviour, to let this poor wretch's soul warm itself near the door."

"It's that Jon," answered Christ. "No, woman; he had no faith in Me."

Just as He said this He was about to shut the door, but the old woman was not slow, far from it—she flung the bag with the soul in it right past him, so that it hurtled far into the halls of Heaven, but then the door was slammed and bolted.

Then a great weight was lifted from the old woman's heart when Jon got into the Kingdom of Heaven in spite of everything, and she went home happy; and we know nothing more about her, nor about what became of Jon's soul after that.

A Tale of Two Old Women

ESKIMO

Two old women once lived together in a little old igloo. Food was always hard for them to get and there came a time when there was nothing left to eat. That night when they went to bed, one of the old women went right to sleep. But the other old woman stayed awake worrying about what they would do for food. All at once she heard a loud thump outside and going out found a caribou lying beside the igloo. Nobody was in sight so she dragged the deer into the stormshed. The other old woman woke up and asked, "Where did you get that caribou?" to which the first replied, "I found it beside the igloo." Then both old women went back to bed and were soon fast asleep.

For a long time the old women had meat to eat, but at length the caribou was all gone and they again faced starvation. The first old woman went to bed as usual and was soon fast asleep. But while she snored the other sat awake worrying. All at once she heard a thump against the igloo and upon going out found another large caribou lying on the snow. Nobody was to be seen, so she dragged it into the stormshed. As she did so, the other old woman rolled over and asked, "Where did you get that deer?" She replied, "I found it just outside our door." Then both women went to bed and were soon sound asleep.

The caribou meat lasted a long time, but as they had nothing else to eat, the time came when it was gone, and for the third time the old women were about to starve. But the first old woman did not give it a thought. She merely crawled into her sleeping-bag and was soon snoring merrily. The other old woman couldn't sleep. She just lay awake worrying about what would happen to them now that they had no more food. Presently she heard a loud thud against the wall. She ran out expecting to find another caribou, but instead, there stood a fine-looking young man.

"I have come to marry you," said the young man. Then he told her to shut her eyes. As she did so, she began to feel young and full of life and all her troubles seemed to leave her.

"Open your eyes and look down at your feet!" commanded the young man. The old woman opened her eyes, and looking down at her feet saw all the things that had made her old lying there. There was her poverty with its ragged clothes, her cares and worries and the wrinkles they had brought. All these she left in the igloo. She was now young and beautiful again.

The young man took her by the hand and together they floated up into the clouds. When they reached the top of the clouds they went through a small hole and emerged into another land. Soon they came to the young man's igloo. When they went in the bride saw stacks of caribou skins and meat in the stormshed. The man was so rich that his wife had nothing at all to worry about.

One day the husband pointed to the hills nearby and said, "Do not go to those hills, for a family lives there whom I do not wish you to see." The wife obeyed her husband very well for a time, but soon she began to look towards the hills and wonder what kind of people lived over there. Finally her curiosity got the better of her, and when her husband was away hunting, she stole away to the hills. There she came to an old igloo, out of which came an ugly girl in ragged and unclean clothes, who beckoned her to enter.

Inside there sat an old, wicked-looking woman who cried out in a shrill voice, "Let me see her face!" When she looked into the wife's face, everything seemed to whirl before the poor woman's eyes. Then everything turned black and she fell upon the floor in a daze. Thereupon the ugly girl took the new clothes from the unconscious woman and clothed her in rags. Then she knelt down and rubbed her ugly face against that of the young woman. Immediately her face, too, became ugly and moreover she became old and nearly blind.

When the wife finally regained her senses the ugly girl led her to the door and pushed her out. Then, groping about blindly, the poor woman stumbled across the tundra to her husband's igloo.

The young hunter had already returned and when his wife came in he knew at once where she had been. "You have disobeyed me, so you must leave," he said severely, and closed the door against her.

The wretched woman now wanted to return to the earth, but she didn't know how to get down from the clouds. At last she thought of a way. First she took a large sealskin bag from the stormshed and got inside it. Then she tied it tight from the inside. When it was ready she began to roll about until at last the huge bag rolled out through the hole in the clouds and floated lightly to earth. The woman crawled out of the bag unhurt, and strange to say, she was again young and beautiful. She at once forgot her sad experience in the cloudland and walked gayly along the beach. She had not gone far when she met a young man who immediately fell in love with her. She agreed to go with him to his home, and in a short time they were happily married. All went well again and she was as happy for a time as she was in cloudland. However, after a while she began to think about her old home and the other old woman with whom she had lived in poverty and wretchedness. Her husband warned her to stay away from the place, but one day when he was away hunting she stole back to the old tumble-down igloo. No sooner had she entered than her nice, new parka changed for a ragged and soiled one; wrinkles came upon her face and her hair turned gray; her back bent and she began to worry. The other old woman woke up as she entered and then rolled over and was soon snoring peacefully. And so the two old women spent the remainder of their days; the one discontented and worrying all the while, the other happy and contented come what may.

The Old Man in the Moon

BURMA

Once there was an old man in a village, and he earned his living by pounding paddy. He had no friend or companion except an old rabbit. The whole day, and part of the night when there was a moon, the old man pounded the paddy, and the old rabbit crouched nearby, eating the chaff that his master threw away.

One moonlit night the old man, while pounding the paddy, said to himself, "It is sheer waste of time sifting the grain from the chaff after pounding. If only I had an old woman with me, she could do the sifting, and also keep me and my rabbit company."

The Moon-goddess heard his words and felt sorry for him. The next day, taking the form of an old woman, she came to the old man and kept him company. The whole day she sifted with a sieve the grain from the chaff, while the old man pounded the paddy. At nightfall, she went back to the sky.

Every day the Moon-goddess changed herself into an old woman and kept the old man and the rabbit company. At nightfall she always went away, for if it was a moonlit night she had to go and look after her moon, and if it was a moonless night the old man did not need her help, as he did not work in the dark.

Weeks went by in this manner, until the old man asked, "Who are you? Why do you go away when night falls?"

The old woman replied that she was the Moon-goddess.

"Take me and my rabbit to your moon," pleaded the old man, "and let us live with you forever, for we are so lonely without you." So the Moon-goddess took the old man and the rabbit to her moon and let them stay with her forever.

When the moon is full, you can see the old man still pounding rice up there, and the rabbit still eating the chaff that the old man throws away.

The Blind Old Woman

AFRICAN-AMERICAN

Anoder man went to marryin' an ol' woman. She didn' have but one laig. An' she couldn' see hyardly. She tol' de servan' to go an' stick her needle in de pos' to de gate. So when dis young man come up, she say, "What dat stickin' up on yon pos' like needle [makin' out she had such good sight]?" When dey gone an' look, was a needle, sure enough. She look out in de yard: "What's dat out in de san'? Dat's a pin." When dey look, dat was a pin, sure enough. So dis young man says, "I t'ink I marry you, all right." Den dey went to work an' dey married. An' after marryen', time come to undress to go to bed. She had but one laig. So dis young man said, "I wouldn' need you." She said, "If you don' leave me, I'll give you a fortune." An' the young man said, "All right." He said, "What will be the fortune?" She said, "I'll give you a box with five handles." An' de five handles was five kicks. An' kicked him out all togeder. He was gone.

The Cure

SYRIA

An old widow had only one son. When he grew to be a man she found him a bride, but she was jealous of her daughter-in-law and began to complain of imaginary sicknesses. Every day she would nag her son and say, "Bring me the doctor, my boy. Let the doctor come." The son did nothing for a while, but eventually he gave in and went to fetch the doctor. While he was out, the widow washed herself and lined her eyes with *kohl.* She put on her best gown and wound a sash of silk about her waist. She donned a velvet vest and her daughter-in-law's wedding headdress and placed an embroidered kerchief over it. Then she sat and waited. When the doctor arrived and asked for his patient, the son showed him in and said, "There she is. It is my mother. Since the moment I was married she has been grumbling like a hen, and not one day has brought her joy or pleasure." "This lady needs a husband," said the doctor. "But she is my mother!" "Yes," said the doctor, "and she needs a groom." "She is over ninety years old! Surely she can't be thinking of marriage again!" "You are wrong, my son," said the doctor. "As often as her skirts are lifted by the wind, the thought of a bridegroom enters her mind." "Sir," said the son, "if she had wanted a husband, she could have married long ago. Why don't you examine her and see what is the matter with her." "I have already told you what is wrong." At this the old woman sprang up from her corner and said to her son, "My boy, may you find favor in the sight of God, do you fancy yourself a greater expert than the wise doctor?"

Notes for Stories

INTRODUCTION

"Old Man, Young Mistress" is a tale from Aesop that settled in the East—both in Arabic countries and in the Orient.

"The Seventh Father of the House," a Norwegian story, is a version of Tale Type 726: "The Oldest on the Farm." There are variants around the world, including one Cajun story, "The Traveler," in which the ninety-year-old man complains, "My father spanked me," and then goes on to tell the narrator that his father is in deep converse over the fence with his grandfather.

"The Old Man and His Grandson," Motif J121, Type 980, has been found in both literary and oral versions all over the world. This is the Grimm story.

"Mountain of Abandoned Old People" can be traced back to eleventh-century Japan. The Ukrainian tale "The Red

Death" (meaning an honorable death) is similar. There is a variant story—in which the old man is taken out of hiding to teach the tribe how to defeat an ogre—told by the Lamda, one of the Bantu tribes of Central Africa. It begins, "One day the chief said to all the people, 'All you young men, bring your fathers and let me kill them. . . .'" And another Japanese story, "The Old Woman on the Mountain," tells the story from a son/old mother point of view. The basic tale has accreted to the King Solomon cycle of stories.

"The Bell of Atri" is a variant of a fourteenth-century Italian fable in which a serpent rings the bell to oust an evil toad from her nest. The blind emperor gives the serpent justice, and in return the serpent gives the emperor a gemstone that cures his blindness. This story can be found in Chinese and Russian lore as well. "The Bell of Atri" bears some similarities to Type 101, in which a faithful old dog, having outlived his usefulness, is to be killed by his master. (See "Old Sultan," Grimm story #48; the Ukrainian "Old Dog Sirko"; and the Aesop story "The Old Hound.")

"The Old Man and Death" is one of the Aesop fables that found its way into the Arabic/Jewish world of stories and from there to Europe. There are many retellings of this short tale, but little variation. The usual variant is that it is an old woman instead of an old man, as in the Czechoslovakian "Death and the Old Gypsy Woman."

"Iron Logic" is one of a number of joke stories that were popular in the Yiddish storytelling tradition. Nathan Ausubel, who collected an enormous number of Jewish stories, has an entire chapter labeled "Jewish Salt," which includes many similar fables.

"One More Gift" is a Japanese story.

"The Two Friends Who Set Off to Travel Round the World" is a typical Eskimo (Inuit) story, with few—if any—European counterparts.

"The Span of Man's Life" is a version of Type 828, "Men and Animals Readjust Span of Life." Variants of the story have been found in Hungary, India, and Lithuania. It is Grimm's #176.

"The Mortal Lord" is a story from the teachings of the great Taoist philosopher Lieh Tzu, from the Chin Dynasty period, third or fourth century A.D.

WISDOM

"An Old Man and a Boy," from East Africa's Kamba people, is a short, pithy "wisdom" tale.

"Empty-Cup Mind" is a Japanese story, attributed to an anecdote told about Zen master Nan-in, who lived in the Meiji period, 1868–1912.

"The Old Woman of the Spring" comes from the Cheyenne people, one of many stories about the gifts of particular foods to a Native American tribe. The "north" in the story is, according to Erdoes and Ortiz, a "nostalgic reference to the Cheyenne hunting grounds in north-central America from which they were driven by invading tribes, probably the Ojibway."

"The Brownie of Blednock," a Scottish story, is about one of the most engaging of Scottish house spirits. Brownies traditionally spun, cleaned, sang babies to sleep, baked, churned butter, and performed a dozen other household chores besides. Only two things could turn a Brownie away from a family it had chosen to serve: trying to pay the Brownie, or criticizing the way it went about its work. The name Aiken-Drum is also found in the popular Scottish folk rhyme "There cam' a man to oor toon." There are a number of popular motifs included in this tale: F381.3, "Fairy leaves when he is given clothes"; F482.5.4, "Helpful deeds of Brownie or other household spirit"; and F382.4, "Opening Holy Bible in presence of fairies nullifies their spells." There are similar or parallel stories in Grimm ("The Shoemaker and the Elves"), in Joseph Jacobs's collection of English stories, and in collections of Norwegian tales.

"The Wise Woman," an Algerian tale, has also been ascribed to medieval sieges in Europe, entering into histories as "true" stories.

"An Old Man Who Saved Some Ungrateful People" comes from Zimbabwe, in Africa. It has clear connections with other Motif J151.1 stories, such as "Mountain of Abandoned People" (above).

"An Old Man's Wisdom" comes from India's Nagaland. Scholars feel it may be an amalgam of a native story and the influence of outsiders—either Christian missionaries or Hindu peasants. This judgment is based on the fact that the story is quite straightforward in its teaching, without supernatural intervention of any kind, the more usual kind of story told by the people of Nagaland.

"Hide Anger Until Tomorrow" is a story from Suriname that is retold by African-Americans. There are parallel stories in the Jewish tradition and in Central America as well.

"The Three Counsels" is clearly a Mexican variation of "Hide Anger Until Tomorrow" (see above) but extends the central story by quite a bit.

"The Truth," from Syria, is one of a group of widely known folk stories about the clever solving of riddles. Folk scholars believe these stories began as literary tales, then moved into the folk culture. This particular story seems closest to Type 921, "The King and the Peasant's Son," wherein a king asks a series of questions/riddles of the boy. The core tale and its variants are Oriental in origin, coming "ultimately from India," according to Stith Thompson. It was transmitted to Jewish storytellers and became part of the King Solomon cycle of tales.

"The Old Man and the Grain of Wheat" is a Russian story that has some similarities to "The Seventh Father of the House" (see above), which is Type 726, "The Oldest on the Farm." But attached to it is a wisdom story.

"Elijah and the Poor Man's Wish," a Jewish story in the Elijah cycle of tales, bears a similarity to the classic "three wishes" stories. The turnabout with the wife's suggesting how to get the best of Elijah's wishes is original to this tale.

"The Wise Man and the Apprentice," a story from Central Asia—Iran and Afghanistan—has parallel stories throughout the Middle East. It also has strong echoes of "The Three Counsels" (see above), where seemingly ridiculous strictures from the wise man turn out to be important when seen from a larger perspective. A related group of stories are Icelandic/Irish/Norwegian: "The Mermaid's Message," ML4060, in which a mermaid (or merman or leprechaun) gives advice that seems nonsensical except from the broader vantage.

"The Poppet Caught a Thief," an American story from the Ozarks, has become part of urban legend as well. It has also found its way to Hollywood, where it has been used as part of a plot in several TV movies.

TRICKERY

"The Clever Old Man" comes from Assam, in India.

"How Grandpa Mowed the Lord's Meadow," a Russian story, is in a long line of "foolish master" stories that were quite popular among the peasantry.

"Kitta Gray" is from Sweden, and one section comes straight out of Aesop, K11.1, Type 1074, except that, instead of Turtle's placing his relatives on the racecourse to fool his opponent, Kitta Gray plays the trick. The ending—the woman in the glass case—is well known enough to have its own tale type, 1170. The story is popular in Scandinavia and the Baltic countries, though not otherwise widely disseminated in Europe.

"The Devil and the Gipsy" is a Russian story that includes a number of folk motifs, including K11.6, Type 1072, the little son who races is a rabbit; K12.2, Type 1071, the wrestling ruse in which Grandfather is a bear. Both these motifs developed in Eastern Europe and attach themselves to many "contest" stories.

"The Old Woman and the Giant" comes from the Philippines. Beginning like a "Three Billy Goats Gruff" variant, it shows its cultural origins by the end of the tale: Beating a gong and making other loud sounds is a surefire way to rid oneself of wicked spirits in the East.

"John Fraser the Cook" is a Scottish version of an old joke that has made its way throughout Europe, Type AT785a, "The Goose with One Leg."

"The Seven Leavenings" is a Palestinian Arab tale whose title comes from a cycle of stories around seven themes, though in this telling there are only two. Its type motif is N825.3, old woman as helper. In this instance, since older women of the culture are thought to be asexual—according to the authors of *Speak, Bird, Speak Again: Palestinian Arab Folktales*—the husband more readily believes her than his own wife.

"The Fortune-Teller" is a Russian folktale that reads like a real scam.

"The Old Woman and the Physician" is from Aesop.

"Two Women Overcome Nez Percé Man" is a Coeur d'Alene story, which can be read as a folktale or as a historical anecdote.

"The Silver Swindle," from China, is a folktale that has been turned into a real scam.

"The Straw Ox" is a Cossack tale that seems to owe a lot to the tar-baby story, a tale that originated in Africa and spread across Europe, as well as through the Americas.

"The Two Old Women's Bet," a story from the southern Appalachians, in America, clearly uses the Hans Christian Andersen story "The Emperor's New Clothes," Type 1406, for part of its plot. Andersen himself leaned heavily on Danish folklore for his stories.

"The Fisherman and the Genie" comes from the *Arabian Nights*. The exchange between the genie and the old man at the end parallels the story of "Puss in Boots," a popular European tale. The *Arabian Nights* version is the older.

"The Five Wolves," a Salishan (Native American) tribal story, is a double *pourquoi* story; it explains why wolves have dark marks at the sides of their mouths, and how the chickadee came to be.

"The Crafty Woman," a Lithuanian story, is related in intent and ending to "Kitta Gray" (above), in which an old woman is slier than the Devil himself.

"The Talking Turkeys," from Syria, is typical of medieval jest stories from the Middle East.

"The Old Woman and the Fox," from India's Bengal province, is a fairly widespread tale. Sometimes the old lady carves out a pumpkin rather than a gourd, and rolls away happily in that.

"Bucca Dhu and Bucca Gwidden" is a Cornish tale, from the southwest corner of England. "Buccas" are mischievous spirits, related to the *poukas* or *phoukas* of Ireland and Scotland and the *bwbachod* of Wales.

ADVENTURE

"Verlioka" is a Russian ogre story that includes the classic gathering of magical objects to defeat the villain. What makes this story unusual is that it deals with a grandfather doing the rescuing, whereas the hero in these tales is usually a boy or girl who is kind and good. "Kisel" is a sourish meat pottage.

"The Lord of Death" is from India's Punjab region. Death or the Devil as a shape-shifter is not a unique idea, nor is the idea of Death personified.

"The Man Who Lodged with Serpents" is from Hungary.

"Kwatee and the Monster in Lake Quinault" is a Native American *pourquoi* story from the Quinault Indians. The lake is on the west side of the Olympic Peninsula, not far from Olympic National Park. Kwatee the Changer is a culture hero.

"Lump Off, Lump On" is from Japan, but there are parallel stories in Ireland—as well as a famous Irish song called "Monday, Tuesday," which tells the same story only with a hump on the back.

"Siksruk, the Witch-Doctor" is an Eskimo story which has shamanistic elements.

"Old Roaney," from the southern Applachians in the United States, has elements of the Baron Münchhausen tall-tale stories. In the Münchhausen version a fox is whipped till it jumps out of its skin.

"The Old Woman and the Rice Cakes" is a Japanese story that has become quite popular in the United States, due in part to its being included in many storytellers' repertoires and the fact that an award-winning children's book was made from it: *The Funny Little Woman* (1972), by Arlene Mosel, with pictures by Blair Lent, won the Caldecott Medal.

"The Poor Countryman and the Greedy Hag" (Type 563, "The Table, the Ass and the Stick") comes from Poland. But the core story has extensive distribution in Europe, Asia, Africa, and both North and South America. The story with most of its essential elements can be traced back to a sixth-century collection of Chinese Buddhist stories.

"St. David's Flood" is from England and is a legend rather than a folktale.

"The Staff of Elijah," part of the great cycle of Elijah stories, is a Jewish story from Moldavia.

"The Magical Words" is Lafcadio Hearn's retelling of a section of the *Kalevala*, the great Finnish hero saga about the god-smiths who first wrought the foundations of the world, and about the witches and enchanters of the North.

"Kalapana" is part of the Hawaiian/Polynesian legendary cycle of heroes. This version was told to Mary Kawena Pukui by a Puna cousin.

"The Great Jaguar" comes from Guatemala and is a Mayan fable.

"The Hunted Hare" is a Celtic story from the southwest of England. "White ladies" were pagan fertility goddesses who had been transmuted into ghosts or fairy creatures. Folklorist Katherine Briggs writes that "the use of White Ladies for both ghosts and fairies is an indication of close connection between fairies and the dead."

"The Apparition of Arran," a Scottish story, was first set down in the nineteenth century and is a legend, rather than a folktale. But there are elements of folklore here: the laying of a ghost, the grateful dead man, and the giving of warnings.

"The Valiant Fish Trapper" comes from Hungary and is one of the most widely told historic legends in that country. It was developed during the years of Turkish occupation (1526–1686).

"Grandmother Spider Steals the Fire" is a Choctaw (Native American) *pourquoi* tale. The Choctaw people lived in what is now Tennessee and Mississippi. While "Grandmother" and "Grandfather" are often simple story honorifics—not necessarily indicating age so much as position and status—in this story Grandmother Spider seems older than the other animals.

"The Monster of Loch Garten" is a local legend that comes from Scotland.

"The Woman in the Moon," a Hawaiian tale, is especially poignant for women who understand Hina's desire, "If only I could go away and find some rest."

"The Hedley Kow," from England, is the tale of an irrepressible optimist. The Hedley Kow is a local form of a bogey, a mischievous though not malevolent spirit. This tale is a variant of Hans Christian Andersen's story "The Goodman Is Always Right."

"The Search for Luck" comes from Greece. It is clearly Type 461 ("Three Hairs from the Devil's Beard"), in which the core story has the hero asking questions of a magical host for those he or she has met upon the way: why a certain tree does not flourish, how a girl avoided by suitors can marry, why a spring has gone dry, and so on. The questions vary, but the story remains. The "Three Hairs" story can be found in some three hundred variants all across Europe; the oldest known version was found on a bit of Assyrian cuneiform.

AND A LITTLE BIT OF LOVE

"Baucis and Philemon," a Greek myth, is considered the classic example of conjugal fidelity. The Roman poet Ovid is the written source—in *Metamorphoses*, Book 8, lines 620–724. Born in 43 B.C., Ovid was both a poet and—at some time—a government official. His *Metamorphoses* is the work from which we take most of our Greek and Roman mythological stories.

"How Much You Remind Me of My Husband!" is an El Salvadoran tale.

"A Clever Old Bride" is a Korean tale, collected in 1913.

"My Jon's Soul" is an Icelandic tale, collected by the Reverend Matthias Jochumsson (d. 1920). In medieval French and German literature, the hero is a farmer arguing with the saints and reminding them of their sins. Only in the Icelandic variant is the Virgin Mary included in the story.

"A Tale of Two Old Women" is an Eskimo story. The warning and the disobedience that follows are similar to those of the Bluebeard stories (Type 956), though the punishment, while severe, is not so dire.

"The Old Man in the Moon" is a Burmese tale. "Pounding paddy" means pounding rice.

"The Blind Old Woman" is an African-American story from Hilton Head, South Carolina, and its energies are exactly opposite to those of "Baucis and Philemon." There is at least one known variant (from Hampton, Virginia) in which the old woman is a pitiable figure. But here she takes charge!

"The Cure" is a story from Syria.

Bibliography

INTRODUCTION

"Old Man, Young Mistress," retold by Jane Yolen, based on Aesop and "The Bald Old Man" from *Folk Tales from Korea,* by Zong In-Sob. New York: Grove Press, 1979.

"The Seventh Father of the House," from *Norwegian Folktales,* by Asbjornson and Moe. New York: Pantheon Books, n.d.

"The Old Man and His Grandson," from *Grimm's Fairy Tales.* London: Routledge & Kegan Paul, 1948.

"Mountain of Abandoned Old People," from *Folk Legends of Japan,* edited by Richard M. Dorson. Tokyo: Charles E. Tuttle Company, n.d.

"The Bell of Atri," from *Fair Is Fair,* retold by Sharon Creeden. Little Rock, Ark.: August House Publishers, 1994.

"The Old Man and Death," retold by Jane Yolen from Thomas James's *Aesop*, 1848.

"Iron Logic," from *A Treasury of Jewish Folklore*, edited by Nathan Ausubel. New York: Crown Publishing, 1948.

"One More Gift," from *Folktales from the Snow Country*, vol. I. Nagaoka English Speaking Society, n.d.

"Tickle me up . . . ," Muriel Rukeyser, from "In Her Burning," from *Out of Silence*. Evanston, Ill.: Triquarterly Books, 1992.

"The Two Friends Who Set Off to Travel Round the World," from *Eskimo Folk-tales*, collected by Knud Rasmussen. Copenhagen: Gyldenal, 1921.

"The Span of Man's Life," from *Folktales of Israel*, by Dov Noy. Chicago: University of Chicago Press, 1963.

"The Mortal Lord," from *Chinese Fairy Tales and Fantasies*, translated and edited by Moss Roberts. New York: Pantheon Books, 1979.

May Sarton, "Now I Become Myself," from *Collected Poems 1930–1993*. New York: W. W. Norton, 1998.

"An Old Man and a Boy," from *East African Folktales: From the Voice of Mukamba,* by Dr. Vincent Muli Wa Kituku. Little Rock, Ark.: August House Publishers, 1997.

"Empty-Cup Mind," from *Wisdom Tales from Around the World,* retold by Heather Forest. Little Rock, Ark.: August House Publishers, 1996.

"The Old Woman of the Spring," from *American Indian Myth and Legends,* selected and edited by Richard Erdoes and Alfonso Ortiz. New York: Pantheon Books, 1984.

"The Brownie of Blednock," from *Children's Tales from Scottish Ballads,* by Elizabeth Grierson. London: A. and C. Black, 1906.

"The Wise Woman," from *Wise Women: Folk and Fairy Tales from Around the World,* retold and edited by Suzanne I. Barchers. Englewood, Colo.: Libraries Unlimited, 1990.

"An Old Man Who Saved Some Ungrateful People," from *Children of Wax,* by Alexander McCall Smith. Edinburgh: Canongate, 1989.

"An Old Man's Wisdom," from *Folktales of India,* edited by Brenda E. F. Beck, Peter J. Claus, Praphulladatta Goswami, and Jawaharlal Handoo. Chicago: University of Chicago Press, 1987.

"Hide Anger Until Tomorrow," from *Afro-American Folktales,* selected and edited by Roger D. Abrahams. New York: Pantheon Books, 1985.

"The Three Counsels," from *Mexican-American Folklore,* compiled and edited by John O. West. Little Rock, Ark.: August House Publishers, 1988.

"The Truth," from *Arab Folktales,* translated and edited by Inea Bushnaq. New York: Penguin Books, n.d.

"The Old Man and the Grain of Wheat," from *New Found Tales from Many Lands,* by Joseph Burke Egan. Philadelphia: John C. Winston Company, 1930.

"Elijah and the Poor Man's Wish," from *Because God Loves Stories: An Anthology of Jewish Storytelling,* edited by Steve Zeitland. New York: Touchstone/Simon & Schuster, 1997.

"The Wise Man and the Apprentice," from *Folk Tales of Central Asia,* by Amina Shah. London: Octagon Press, 1970.

"The Poppet Caught a Thief," from *Wise Women,* retold and edited by Suzanne I. Barchers. Englewood, Colo.: Libraries Unlimited, 1990.

TRICKERY

"The Clever Old Man," from *Folktales of India*, edited by Brenda E. F. Beck, Peter J. Claus, Praphulladatta Goswami, and Jawaharlal Handoo. Chicago: University of Chicago Press, 1987.

"How Grandpa Mowed the Lord's Meadow," from *The Twelve Clever Brothers and Other Fools: Folktales from Russia*, collected and adapted by Mirra Ginsburg. New York: J. B. Lippincott, 1979.

"Kitta Gray," from *Swedish Folktales and Legends*, selected, translated, and edited by Lone Thygesen Blecher and George Blecher. New York: Pantheon Books, 1993.

"The Devil and the Gipsy," from *Folk Tales of All Nations*, edited by F. H. Lee. New York: Coward-McCann, 1932.

"The Old Woman and the Giant," from *Tales from the Mountain Province*. Manila: Philippine Education Co., 1958.

"John Fraser the Cook," from *The Penguin Book of Scottish Folktales*, edited by Neil Philip. London: Penguin Books, 1995.

"The Seven Leavenings," from *Speak, Bird, Speak Again: Palestinian Arab Folktales*, by Ibrahim Muhawi and Sharif Kanaana. Berkeley: University of California Press, 1989.

"The Fortune-Teller," from *The Three Kingdoms: Russian Tales from Alexander Afanasiev's Collection*. Moscow: Raduga Publishers, 1985.

"The Old Woman and the Physician," from *Fables: Aesop and Others.* London: J. M. Dent & Sons, 1913; and New York: E. P. Dutton, 1936.

"Two Women Overcome Nez Percé Man," from *An Analysis of Coeur d'Alene Indian Myths,* by Gladys A. Reichard. Philadelphia: American Folklore Society, 1947.

"The Silver Swindle," from *Chinese Fairy Tales and Fantasies,* translated and edited by Moss Roberts. New York: Pantheon Books, 1979.

"The Straw Ox," from *Folk Tales of All Nations,* edited by F. H. Lee. New York: Coward-McCann, 1932.

"The Two Old Women's Bet," from *Grandfather Tales,* collected and retold by Richard Chase. Boston: Houghton Mifflin, 1948, 1976.

"The Fisherman and the Genie," from *Best-Loved Folktales of the World,* selected and with an introduction by Joanna Cole. Garden City, N.Y.: Anchor Press/Doubleday, 1983.

"The Five Wolves," from *Folk-Tales of Salishan and Sahaptin Tribes,* collected by James A. Teit, Marian K. Gould, Livingston Farrand, and Herbert J. Spinden, edited by Franz Boas. Lancaster, Pa.: New York: The American Folk-Lore Society, 1917; reprinted, New York: Kraus Reprint Co., 1969.

"The Crafty Woman," from *Siberian and Other Folktales: Primitive Literature of the Empire of the Tsars,* collected and translated by C. Fillingham Coxwell. C. W. Daniel Company, 1925.

"The Talking Turkeys," from *Arab Folktales,* translated and edited by Inea Bushnaq. New York: Penguin Books, n.d.

"The Old Woman and the Fox," from *The Demon Slayers and Other Stories: Bengali Folk Tales,* collected and written by Sayantani DasGupta and Shamita Das Dasgupta. New York: Interlink Books, 1995.

"Bucca Dhu and Bucca Gwidden," from *Tatterhood and Other Tales,* edited by Ethel Johnston Phelps. New York: Feminist Press, n.d.

ADVENTURE

"Verlioka," from *Folk Tales of All Nations,* edited by F. H. Lee. New York: Coward-McCann, 1932.

"The Lord of Death," from *Folktales from India: A Selection of Oral Tales from Twenty-two Languages,* selected and edited by A. K. Ramanujan. New York: Pantheon Books, 1991.

"The Man Who Lodged with Serpents," from *Folktales of Hungary,* edited by Linda Degh. Chicago: University of Chicago Press, 1965.

"Kwatee and the Monster in Lake Quinault," from *Indian Legends of the Pacific Northwest*, by Ella E. Clark. Berkeley: University of California Press, 1953.

"Lump Off, Lump On," from *Japanese Tales*, selected, edited, and translated by Royall Tyler. New York: Pantheon Books, 1987.

"Siksruk, the Witch-Doctor," from *Alaskan Igloo Tales*, by Edward L. Keithahn. Anchorage: Alaska Northwest Publishing Company, n.d.

"Old Roaney," from *Grandfather Tales*, collected and retold by Richard Chase. Boston: Houghton Mifflin, 1948, 1976.

"The Old Woman and the Rice Cakes," from *The Maid of the North: Feminist Folk Tales from Around the World*, by Ethel Johnston Phelps. New York: Holt, Rinehart and Winston, 1981.

"The Poor Countryman and the Greedy Hag," from *The Glass Mountain: Twenty-six Ancient Polish Folktales and Fables*, selected by W. S. Kuniczak. New York: Hippocrene Books, 1992.

"St. David's Flood," from *Wise Women*, retold and edited by Suzanne I. Barchers. Englewood, Colo.: Libraries Unlimited, 1990.

"The Staff of Elijah," from *Miriam's Tambourine: Jewish Folktales from Around the World*, selected and retold by Howard Schwartz. New York: Oxford University Press, 1988.

"The Magical Words," from *Stray Leaves from Strange Literature*, by Lafcadio Hearn. Boston: Houghton Mifflin, 1884.

"Kalapana," from *Pikoi and Other Legends of the Island of Hawaii*, collected or suggested by Mary Kawena Pukui, retold by Caroline Curtis. Honolulu: Kamehameha Schools Press, 1949.

"The Great Jaguar," from *The Bird Who Cleans the World and Other Mayan Fables*, collected by Victor Montejo, translated by Wallace Kaufman. Willimantic, Conn.: Curbstone Press, 1992.

"The Hunted Hare," from *Tatterhood and Other Tales*, edited by Ethel Johnston Phelps. New York: Feminist Press, n.d.

"The Apparition of Arran," from *The Penguin Book of Scottish Folktales*, edited by Neil Philip. London: Penguin Books, n.d.

"The Valiant Fish Trapper," from *Folktales of Hungary*, edited by Linda Degh. Chicago: University of Chicago Press, 1965.

"Grandmother Spider Steals the Fire," from *Race with Buffalo: And Other Native American Stories for Young Readers*, collected and edited by Richard Young, and Judy Dockrey Young. Little Rock, Ark.: August House Publishers, 1994.

"The Monster of Loch Garten," from *Selected Highland Folk Tales*, gathered orally by Ronald Mcdonald Robertson. Essex, England: Oliver and Boyd, 1961.

"The Woman in the Moon," from *Wise Women*, retold and edited by Suzanne I. Barchers. Englewood, Colo.: Libraries Unlimited, 1990.

"The Hedley Kow," from *More English Fairy Tales*, Joseph Jacobs. 1894. New York: Schocken, 1968.

"The Search for Luck," from *Modern Greek Folktales*, chosen and translated by R. M. Dawkins. Oxford: Oxford University Press, 1953.

AND A LITTLE BIT OF LOVE
"Baucis and Philemon," from *Bulfinch's Mythology: The Age of Fable*. New York: Doubleday, 1968.

"How Much You Remind Me of My Husband!" from *The King of the Mountains: A Treasury of Latin American Folk Stories*, retold by M. A. Jagendorf and R. S. Boggs. New York: Vanguard Press, 1960.

"A Clever Old Bride," from *Folk Tales from Korea*, by Zong In-Sob. New York: Grove Press, 1979.

"My Jon's Soul," from *Icelandic Folktales and Legends*, by Jacqueline Simpson. Berkeley: University of California Press, 1972.

"A Tale of Two Old Women," from *Alaskan Igloo Tales*, compiled by Edward L. Keithahn. Anchorage: Alaska Northwest Publishing Company, 1974.

"The Old Man in the Moon," from *A Kingdom Lost for a Drop of Honey,* by Maung Htin Aung and Helen G. Trager. New York: Parents Magazine Press, 1968.

"The Blind Old Woman," from *Folk-Lore of the South Sea Island, South Carolina,* by Elsie Clews Parsons. Cambridge, Mass.: American Folk-Lore Society, 1923.

"The Cure," from *Arab Folktales,* translated and edited by Inea Bushnaq. New York: Penguin Books, n.d.

Index of Titles

FOR THE BEST IN PAPERBACKS, LOOK FOR THE

In every corner of the world, on every subject under the sun, Penguin represents quality and variety—the very best in publishing today.

For complete information about books available from Penguin—including Puffins, Penguin Classics, and Arkana—and how to order them, write to us at the appropriate address below. Please note that for copyright reasons the selection of books varies from country to country.

In the United Kingdom: Please write to *Dept. JC, Penguin Books Ltd, FREEPOST, West Drayton, Middlesex UB7 0BR.*

If you have any difficulty in obtaining a title, please send your order with the correct money, plus ten percent for postage and packaging, to *P.O. Box No. 11, West Drayton, Middlesex UB7 0BR*

In the United States: Please write to *Consumer Sales, Penguin USA, P.O. Box 999, Dept. 17109, Bergenfield, New Jersey 07621-0120.* VISA and MasterCard holders call 1-800-253-6476 to order all Penguin titles

In Canada: Please write to *Penguin Books Canada Ltd, 10 Alcorn Avenue, Suite 300, Toronto, Ontario M4V 3B2*

In Australia: Please write to *Penguin Books Australia Ltd, P.O. Box 257, Ringwood, Victoria 3134*

In New Zealand: Please write to *Penguin Books (NZ) Ltd, Private Bag 102902, North Shore Mail Centre, Auckland 10*

In India: Please write to *Penguin Books India Pvt Ltd, 706 Eros Apartments, 56 Nehru Place, New Delhi 110 019*

In the Netherlands: Please write to *Penguin Books Netherlands bv, Postbus 3507, NL-1001 AH Amsterdam*

In Germany: Please write to *Penguin Books Deutschland GmbH, Metzlerstrasse 26, 60594 Frankfurt am Main*

In Spain: Please write to *Penguin Books S. A., Bravo Murillo 19, 1° B, 28015 Madrid*

In Italy: Please write to *Penguin Italia s.r.l., Via Felice Casati 20, I-20124 Milano*

In France: Please write to *Penguin France S. A., 17 rue Lejeune, F-31000 Toulouse*

In Japan: Please write to *Penguin Books Japan, Ishikiribashi Building, 2-5-4, Suido, Bunkyo-ku, Tokyo 112*

In Greece: Please write to *Penguin Hellas Ltd, Dimocritou 3, GR-106 71 Athens*

In South Africa: Please write to *Longman Penguin Southern Africa (Pty) Ltd, Private Bag X08, Bertsham 2013*